The Born-Again Phoenix

The Born-Again Phoenix

The Birken Saga—Book 3

Harald Lutz

BRUCKNER

Books by Harald Lutz Bruckner

The Blue Sapphire Amulet

The Birken Saga
A Trilogy

Book 1 *Escape on the Astral Express*
Book 2 *A Wanderer on the Earth*
Book 3 *The Born-Again Phoenix*

For Matt and Mary

1965–1974

Chapter 1

IN the third week of the fall quarter of 1965 at Wayne State University, Hektor walked into his classroom at seven forty-five and sat down in the front row. He was about to write his very first exam in an English-speaking country. Hektor had never attended school in the United States or taken any kind of exam other than his GED the first year, the citizenship tests in 1960, and the recent college entrance exams.

He opened his blank blue book and made sure all his pencils were sharpened. The course in question dealt with ancient history; the anticipated subject for the test was aspects of the Law Code of Hammurabi. He had read and studied extensively in preparation for this first major event in the new course of direction he had chosen. Hektor felt confident as he waited for the start of the test. His professor walked in promptly at eight o'clock and passed out the feared questions. Hektor took one look at them and panicked.

What's this all about? Where did I see that name before? Who is Hammurabi? It was like a curtain had been drawn, wiping away all that was stored in his thirty-one-year-old brain. Everyone around him was frantically writing while Hektor sat quietly staring into space, at the blue book in front of him, or at his teacher. After twenty minutes, the professor walked over to speak to him.

"Why aren't you writing? I am quite aware of what you know and what you should be able to write. Aren't you feeling well, Mr. Birken?"

"I feel just fine; the only problem is that I can't remember a thing about the subject at hand. I've drawn a complete blank. Sorry to disappoint you."

The teacher returned to his desk, his body language conveyed total disbelief in what he was observing. He kept glancing at Hektor every few minutes, hoping that Hektor would make some kind of an attempt at answering a question or two. He waited in vain; it didn't happen. After fifty minutes, Hektor turned in a blank blue book. His professor opened the exam and merely stood there, shook his head, and shrugged his shoulders.

"Now I've seen it all," he mumbled as he tucked the exam papers into his briefcase.

Hektor walked to his next lecture like a zombie. He was half tempted to head straight for the garage and drive home. He was convinced his American college career was short-lived. Mr. Late Bloomer couldn't help seeing a public telephone and was ready to call Bob Mitchell and ask for reinstatement to his job at Tip-Top. But then, he knew better than to do anything rash and wanted first to discuss his testing debacle with Laura. After his last lecture, he walked up to the GM building and stopped by her office. They sat down in one of the conference rooms and stared at each other. Laura looked at him in complete disbelief. Uncharacteristically, Hektor was totally deflated. He finally spoke up.

"I can tell by your eyes; you don't have to say a word. You keep asking me what happened. I drew a total blank and didn't write a single word. It was almost like I had a stroke—and it wasn't a stroke of genius. Talk about making a big mistake; I feel like a complete ass.

I'm really tempted to call Bob and beg him to take me back. This isn't going to work for me."

"Oh, no!" Laura replied. "We are not giving up this easily. I remember you often telling me that you've never started anything in life you haven't finished. This is one of those starts—and you will finish it. You know the expression 'talking like a Dutch uncle'? Well, let me tell you something, mister: I'm talking to you like a Dutch aunt. You make an appointment with that Hammurabi professor and see if he will give you a makeup exam.

"And if not, you'll just plan on doing a heck of a lot better for the remainder of the quarter. This is one time that I'll insist on you trying harder and doing well in the end. And don't give me that nonsense about being too old to learn new things. Put that in your pipe and smoke it."

He could tell Laura was angry; Hektor saw a side of her he had never encountered before. It was clearly a case of a strong woman behind every successful man.

Subsequently, Hektor did well on all exams and ended with a 3.65 GPA for the three classes he was taking during his first quarter. A professor in the Humanities Center became his advisor. He encouraged Hektor to pursue a degree in comparative literature, English/German, allowing him to take advantage of his extensive knowledge of German and the works of its many well-known literary greats.

※

After the successful completion of the first quarter, Hektor believed it was high time for him to find some sort of part-time employment. He felt guilty letting Laura shoulder all of their financial responsibilities. She wasn't sure if this was the right time for him to find work.

"I'm not certain you should spread yourself this thin at this point. Just because you managed to come out on top during the first quarter doesn't mean things will be much easier from now on. I believe you are making a mistake."

"Well, let me make my own mistakes. I cannot allow you to be the only breadwinner in this family. I need to make some contribution toward keeping this ship afloat. It can't all rest on your shoulders alone." A search in the want ads of the *Detroit Free Press* was the first step. He found exactly what he was looking for. The small company was conveniently located halfway between home and school.

"Laura, this job sounds perfect for what I want. I have to put in twenty hours a week and can work anytime—day or night. There's total flexibility to my being there. I'm going to call and make an appointment."

Mrs. Dorato was a charming and efficient businesswoman. She and her husband and one other employee basically ran the whole operation. During the interview, Hektor realized that Mrs. Dorato was not exactly a spring chicken. While she had flawless skin and was attractively made up, he could tell that her dark hair had clearly been helped by a dose from a bottle of dye. He liked her smile and the twinkle in her eyes.

"You have excellent recommendations, and I do admire your efforts at returning to studies at this stage in your life. That took guts. More power to you. If you decide to take the job, you will have keys to this place and access to the alarm codes. You may come early in the morning before anyone is here and work as many hours as you choose before heading out to your first class and/or return in the afternoon when it is convenient. There may be days when you have too many classes and cannot come at all. You pick the days and times that fit your schedule best. What do you say?"

"Sounds like a winner to me," said Hektor. "You are a pretty trusting person to hand me keys and security codes right from the start."

"Mr. Birken, you are not some irresponsible kid. You have impeccable credentials and are obviously overqualified for the job. Nevertheless, I appreciate your interest in working and wanting to make a contribution to the well-being of your family. My husband and I are hard-working people and are impressed with what you are trying to do."

"When would you like me to start?"

"How about right now? I'll take you into the stock area and show you what some of your responsibilities might be. There will be crates and boxes needing unpacking and breakable items requiring proper storage in specific sections. I hope you are not afraid to use ladders?"

"No problem; ladders will be fine." They walked into a room filled with jars and little boxes, a tiny scale, and shipping materials.

"There may be times when you will need to fill orders in this room where we keep all our china paints. Other times, you will work in the front and help us with getting catalogs and mailings out to our many customers. On occasion, you might even wait on a customer in the store. I'm glad the hourly wage was acceptable to you. My husband and I look forward to having you with us."

Hektor started working and quickly picked up on what was expected of him. While he got along well with the owners, there were tense moments between him and the one and only other employee, Ludovico. For some idiotic reason, the Oriental gentleman appeared to be threatened by the newcomer.

After six months on the job, one Friday morning the store was brimming with chattering women all excited about the latest china blanks advertised in the most recent mailing of the catalog. Mrs. Dorato stepped into the stockroom and asked Hektor to serve some of the anxious clients waiting to be helped in the store. Ludovico was great, laying on the schmaltz in that syrupy voice of his when he could take all the time in the world and tend to a single customer. However, crowd control was clearly not his forté.

Hektor had gotten to know some of the regulars by taking their orders over the phone; these ladies were pleased to make the acquaintance of that unknown face at last. He could tell that Ludovico was not exactly thrilled with the reception Hektor received. *It's great to be exposed to some daylight and mingle with people; I enjoy helping out in a pinch.*

As soon as things settled down, Hektor and Ludovico had their first showdown. The Doratos had gone out to lunch, and Ludovico was brazen enough to confront Hektor.

"I believe it is high time for you to return to the jobs for which you were hired. Put your apron back on and disappear to the stock-room where you belong. I don't need you in the store. This is my domain, and I intend to keep it that way!" Hektor was ready to give the guy a fat lip.

"Whoa! Whoa! You remember who summoned me to work in the store this morning. Let me set you straight, buster. You may have worked here for a few years, but I will not take that kind of crap from you. You are not talking to some kid you can bamboozle. I have abso-lutely no interest in usurping your precious territory. I have bigger fish to fry! If you make another remark like that, I'll discuss the matter with Mr. and Mrs. Dorato."

Hektor walked away giving him the finger; he had no intention of taking the matter any further for now. He could tell by Ludovico's demeanor and facial expressions that he understood what Hektor tried to make perfectly clear. In the course of the almost three years Hektor worked for the Doratos, there were occasional spats; but Ludovico learned his lesson well and never again addressed Hektor in such a demeaning tone.

To Hektor the employment was a convenient means of supple-menting their weekly income. He succeeded in doing so and did it on his own terms. Hektor and Ludovico learned to coexist peacefully and did their respective jobs.

At the end of his first year at WSU, he received a Wayne State University Board of Governors Scholarship for his entire undergraduate work; that is, even his tuition for his first year was refunded. It was found money. He opted for a very special surprise. On her next buying trip to Germany, Mrs. Dorato bought an exceptionally beautiful Hutschenreuther complete service for six and all serving dishes. The factory shipped the order directly to the store. Hektor carefully unpacked his treasure and smuggled his surprise into their home. It was fully on display in their china cabinet when Laura first laid eyes on it.

"What's this? Where did you get it? Where did you get the money to pay for all this?"

"No, I didn't rob the Doratos. I used the money I was refunded from WSU; they gave me back my tuition for the first year. I wanted us to have something beautiful to reward us for what we have achieved during this challenging year. Let's consider it an early Christmas present to each other. Just think, I might have spent the money on a huge artificial Christmas tree."

"Oh, let's not even talk about that. I still have the events associated with our first two natural Christmas trees in front of my eyes. How could I forget you bending the tree stand to straighten out the crooked tree we bought one dark night in 1963 or you angrily tossing the whole tree off the balcony when you couldn't fit it into the stand?

"I was thrilled when you gave up on natural trees after that unforgettable episode last year and bought that beautiful, bargain-priced, artificial tree right after Christmas. Thanks, but no thanks; one tree will do us for now! And—thank you. I love what you have done; these dishes are priceless. I never thought we'd have anything this beautiful so soon."

The studies in the humanities opened his eyes to the worlds of art and music that would enhance his life for the rest of his days. As hard as he tried, he couldn't avoid having to suffer through a science sequence. Eventually he settled on geology, the least invasive and challenging. By testing out of many general education courses, Hektor was able to save one year and received his BA in June 1968.

One of the unexpected perks of being a humanities major was ease of access to very reasonable tickets to many cultural events in the city. The highlight of the spring 1967 quarter was the week-long appearance of the Metropolitan Opera at the Masonic Temple in Detroit. Hektor thought he had died and gone to heaven. Through his professor of music appreciation, he garnered tickets for all seven performances. It was Laura's baptism by fire into the world of opera. Prior to that week, her only exposure to opera had been a performance of *Carmen* when she attended college, the lead being sung by no other than Beverly Sills.

Opening night was *Un Ballo in Maschera* with Leontyne Price as Amelia. The evening began with a humorous event in the auditorium. Moments before the lights were dimmed, an elderly gentleman and a lady in white walked down the aisle to take their seats in the expensive orchestra section. The lady called attention to herself with a dress that flared out dramatically at the bottom. It was the tight fit of the dress that caught the attention of many a gentleman who trained his opera glasses on the appearance of the latecomer.

Laura had learned a few phrases from a self-study book in beginning German. During the first intermission, friends of theirs and Laura and Hektor couldn't believe their eyes when the lady and gentleman in question walked toward them. Laura took a deep breath.

"Aber die Blonde ist hässlich!" [But the blonde is so ugly!], she uttered distinctly to everyone's surprise.

On close inspection, the lady was at least seventy and perhaps older, trying to look twenty-seven or younger. The makeup appeared to have been applied with a spatula; the woman looked almost grotesque. It was indeed comic relief from the seriousness of the operatic plot.

Elisabeth Grümmer sang Elsa in *Lohengrin* the next night. The high points for Laura were the performances by Birgit Nilsson, Franco Corelli, and Renata Scotto in *Turandot* and Franco Corelli and Mirella Freni in *Romeo and Juliet*. For Laura it was indeed a tour de force, working all day at her job and looking perky and appreciative of seven performances in a row. Nevertheless, she showed enthusiasm for an art form to which she had little prior exposure. For Hektor, it was "glory" from start to finish.

Hektor pursued his Master of Arts in German and French nineteenth- and twentieth-century literature and obtained his degree June 1969. His graduate assistantship allowed him to teach various sections of German. The interactions with students in his classes gave him the pleasure he had always dreamed about as a young man. The classroom had alas become his stage. His MA advisor encouraged him to go for his PhD in modern languages; he was accepted into the Department of Germanic Languages and Literatures at the University of Michigan with studies to commence in the fall of 1970.

But this was fall 1969. Hektor's teaching contract at WSU commenced in September. He believed he much needed a break from the intense studies he had pursued for the last four years. Teaching his three classes in beginning and intermediate German was pure joy for the new man among the established faculty. Many of his former professors were only too willing to provide helpful hints to make the process as productive, meaningful, and pleasurable for his students and him.

It had been four years since the Birkens benefited from two regular incomes, and Hektor wanted to show Laura his appreciation for all she had done.

"Have you taken a close look at that 'good' winter coat of yours lately?" Laura looked quizzically at Hektor.

"What do you mean? Don't you like my black coat anymore, or have I outgrown it?"

"Neither. It simply looks tired and is in need of replacing. I want to take you shopping on Saturday. And I don't want any arguments and talk of frivolity. You deserve it."

She had no idea he had bought her a beautiful diamond he intended to present to her under the Christmas tree. He believed it was high time after being married to Laura for almost seven years. She, on the other hand, was perfectly happy with her simple Lohengrin ring of fourteen-carat gold. They parked the car and walked over to Woodward Ave. Having worked in downtown Detroit, Laura was familiar with most of the better stores and their locations.

"Aren't we going to Hudson's? It's in the opposite direction."

"No, honey. We are going to that little fur salon where I bought you that stole for the beautiful Fielding wedding we attended a few years ago."

"Are you nuts? I don't need a fur coat; a nice wool coat will do just fine."

"Let me be the judge of that. I know exactly what I want to get for you." The friendly owner of the shop, Maurice, remembered Hektor and Laura.

"How nice to see you again! What can we do for you today? Do you have anything particular in mind?" Hektor took over.

"I have been eying that beautiful black broadtail coat with the stunning mink collar in the window. I would like my wife to try it on."

"No problem." He took a quick glance at Laura and decided it might be just the right size for her.

"Here we are. Let me slip it on you. Of course, if it isn't perfect, the crew and I know how to make adjustments." Laura held her breath and didn't say a word as she admired the coat, looking at her mirrored reflection. Tears were creeping down her cheeks.

"It's beautiful but much too costly and precious for me. I never dreamed of having a fur coat. I can't get over how light in weight it feels. I always thought Persian lamb was heavier."

"Honey, if I may call you that, it's broadtail, which is much lighter. How does it feel to you otherwise? The only change I see is a slight adjustment in the length of the sleeves. I suggest we give it a pretty cuff-like treatment, which would clearly add to the beauty of the coat," suggested Maurice.

"You got yourself a deal. I would like Laura to try on one of those matching mink hats that I see in the cabinet over there." Laura decided not to make any waves. She had learned over the years to accept her husband's spontaneity when it came to periodic splurges that involved her. He often encouraged her to learn to *live, live, live!*

"Laura, that hat looks great on you. My God, you look like Lara in *Dr. Zhivago*. We'll take it. When will you have the coat ready?"

"It's early enough in the day. We can have the coat ready for you in two hours. You have any other shopping to do?"

"As a matter of fact we do. After shopping for boots and a purse, we'll have lunch at Hudson's. They feature one of my favorite things. Their Maurice Salad is outstanding. It isn't by any chance named after you, is it?"

"No, no. It must have been some other lucky Maurice. But I know what you mean about that salad; it's one of my favorites as well. See you at three thirty. It will all be ready for your pickup. It's been a pleasure doing business again." Maurice was holding the door open for them to leave. They walked out onto Woodward Avenue, with Laura hanging onto Hektor's right arm tightly and smiling like a Cheshire cat.

"You are something else. Thank you, thank you! I'll love wearing my new coat and hat to church on Sunday." At Crowleys, he couldn't resist buying a stunning alligator bag and beautiful black boots at Hudson's.

"Let's go and enjoy our lunch." The salad was as enjoyable as ever. Maurice kept his word; the coat and hat were ready when they stopped at the salon after lunch. Laura decided it was time for her to plan a little surprise for Hektor.

"Before we head home, I would like you to drive over to Grand Boulevard. There is a painting I've been admiring in that charming little boutique gallery near my office. It reminds me so much of the idyllic oil landscape in Greta's dining room. I know you always were fond of it."

"So now you want to have your kind of shopping spree to get even with me, huh?"

"I won't get even with you. I don't believe its price will match anything you spent earlier in the day. But indulge me, and let's at least look at it." The painting was still in the window although Hektor didn't care at all for the framing. It didn't do anything for the beautifully executed work.

"Well, let me find out what the damage might be." They were greeted by a friendly gentleman, perhaps old enough to be their grandfather.

"We like the landscape featured in your window but don't care for the frame; it just wouldn't work with the rest of our décor."

"That's no problem. It's a stretched canvas we can pop out. I'll give you a good price without the frame. You can select a different frame or buy it without any frame. The price for the painting is two hundred dollars. What do you say?" Laura was ready to jump at the offer, but Hektor hesitated for a moment. He had learned to deal in certain situations.

"Thanks for the offer; I would like to think about it. We'll stop in next week after I pick up my wife at GM. We drive by your gallery five days a week."

A friendly handshake and they left the kind old gentleman standing there wondering. He didn't quite get it when Laura winked at him as she marched out of the gallery clinging to Hektor's arm. He turned to Laura.

"It's a nice painting. But let me see if I can get him to come down a few bucks. Some starving artist might accept a little less."

"Why do you need to dicker with the man? It's certainly something I would never have done. I thought his price was fair. You suit yourself. "

"I will, I will. Don't give it another thought."

They drove home and enjoyed the rest of the fall weekend. Laura was a vision in her new duds when they went to church on Sunday. As he drove her to the office on Monday morning, the landscape was back in the window. He had no time to stop back before Wednesday of that week and had the shock of his life as he walked up to the gallery on that afternoon after he had taught his last class.

"Sorry, sir. The painting is gone. A lady came in yesterday afternoon and bought it the way it was, frame and all. May I show you some similar paintings by the artist?"

"No, thank you. The other one reminded us so much of a painting a dear friend in Germany has enjoyed for years. Perhaps some other time." He walked back to the car. When Laura joined him a few minutes later, he couldn't wait to tell her what happened.

"That's too bad. I wish you had let me buy it for you on Saturday." She just giggled to herself.

⋈

Come Thanksgiving, he couldn't stand to sit on his other surprise any longer. He decided to give Laura the long-overdue diamond at the traditional family feast at her parents' home. No one was more shocked than Laura.

"When did you do this? And it even fits perfectly." She kept holding it against the light, mesmerized by the sparkle on her left hand.

"Boy, you really know how to surprise a girl. Thanks, I love it!" Caitlin smiled at Hektor; she had been in on the deal.

X

It was mid-December, and Hektor sat in his office reading final exams for his students. He had closed his office door. His shoes kicked off, he propped up his stockinged feet on his desk. He was totally absorbed in reading his students' papers when the phone disrupted his train of thought. *Who the hell is breaking the spell of the moment?* There was a touch of annoyance in his voice as he lifted the phone off the cradle.

"Hektor Birken, how may I help you?"

"Hi Hektor, it's Evelyne at the office. I've got bad news. Laura wasn't feeling well and had to be taken to Harper Hospital. They are not sure but thought she might have had a mild stroke. Can you get away from the office and hightail it over there? After you see Laura and speak with the doctors, please call me—anytime. I'm really worried. Josef and I will keep her in our prayers." She hung up, realizing what must be running through Hektor's mind.

He was on his way to Harper Hospital within seconds, briefly informing his next-door colleague where he was headed. He was glad to see Laura bedded in a private room thanks to GM's generous healthcare plan. Laura smiled as he walked in the room.

"Sorry, Honey, I hadn't planned this as a last-minute Christmas surprise. I seem to be much better; they gave me some kind of injection. The doctors attending me here and Dr. Humburg want to speak with us ASAP. Right now, all I want to do is close my eyes and sleep. Sorry, I'm not great company." Stepping out of Laura's hospital room, he was greeted by their family physician.

"Let's grab a cup of coffee in the cafeteria. I'll fill you in on what happened. From what the initial assessments show, Laura will be OK and make a full recovery." Hektor walked next to Dr. Humburg without saying a word. He needed to digest all that had transpired in the last few hours.

"Apparently Laura was totally disoriented trying to get on the correct elevator. Most of the operators knew her and got her to the Gold Coast OK, because she often had worked on the floor where the financial staff executive offices were located. Once she arrived, she had no idea who she was or what she was supposed to do. One of the big bosses called her office and spoke with her cohort, Evelyne. She is the person who ordered the ambulance that took Laura to Harper. She's in good hands.

"It appears she had a mild stroke that primarily affected her occipital lobe, thus causing the disorientation and visual problems. The quick intervention will preclude further damage. There are two things that I recommend. Laura should not continue with her birth control regimen and should give up smoking completely. The first might bring about a change in your family constellation, the second will be tough on her day-to-day well-being. I believe Laura should never again subject herself to any sort of hormone-related treatments."

"I agree. Giving up smoking will not be easy, but she'll do it. As far as going off the pill, she won't have a problem with that at all. She has wanted to have children for some time. We'll give it a whirl. Thanks for speaking with me." They shook hands, and the good doctor was on his way to consult with other patients. Hektor called Evelyne to give her the news.

"Boy, giving up smoking will be tough on Laura; I remember the last time she tried that. She was hell on wheels. As much as I wanted her to quit, I reached the conclusion that she was better off smoking than being so traumatically impacted by the absence of her nicotine fixes. Gosh, I might become a godmother!" Evelyne let it rest there.

Hektor took Laura home two days before Christmas. Once she was settled comfortably in the Impala, Laura spoke up.

"I have a little surprise for you. It was supposed to work differently, but under the circumstances, you must claim the present yourself." As they were passing the little gallery on Grand Boulevard, she gently nudged him with her left elbow.

"Please stop and see the old gentleman. He's waiting for you with a Christmas present."

"You're kidding, aren't you?"

"No, I was the lady who bought the painting. I asked the old gent to be in on the surprise and to tell you that it was sold just the way it was. I only bought the painting, not the frame you didn't like. It's all paid for. He'll have a good laugh when you walk in. I spoke with him on the phone from the hospital. He knows why I couldn't pick it up myself."

⋊⋉

"Nice to see you, young man." He smiled from ear to ear.

"Hope you will enjoy this lovely painting your wife bought. I was happy to be in on the little deceptive games she was playing with you." They shook hands, and Hektor walked out with his treasure all wrapped in beautiful Christmas foil. Laura laughed out loud as he got in next to her and planted a soft kiss on her lips.

"Thank you; that was sweet of you!"

"You are most welcome, Sir Hektor. And Merry Christmas!"

Hektor had put up their beautiful, although artificial, tree and the house was completely decorated for Christmas. Nevertheless, the holiday spirits were somewhat subdued since Laura was still not completely herself. It took several weeks before she was ready to return to work. What they did enjoy were their moments of extreme closeness in their efforts to conceive a child.

For now, the oil painting was stored in their bedroom closet. Hektor had it appropriately framed and presented it to Laura for her twenty-eighth birthday the following June.

Chapter 2

AFTER the first of the year, Laura encouraged Hektor to attend a Modern Language Association (MLA) conference, allowing him to scout out future job opportunities in his chosen field. He walked around the conference center and spoke with many prospective employers. Hektor was beginning to think they were playing a recorded message.

"As you can tell, we are not the only institution *not* looking for anyone with a terminal degree in Germanic languages. We have openings in Russian, Chinese, and some of the classic languages. Is it too late for you to consider a different track?"

He heard the same thing over and over and was terribly disappointed, and yet he was glad that he went. The experience opened his eyes to the possibility of not finding suitable employment once he attained his union card four years hence. Most doctoral candidates jokingly spoke of their PhD diplomas as being the union card guaranteeing them a job in academia. When Laura picked him up at the airport, she knew right away that things hadn't gone well. She touched his face and then gave him a kiss after he got into the car.

"What's wrong? You look like you've lost your best friend."

"Really? Is it that obvious? Let's go home, have a glass of wine, and talk."

"It's that bad? I can't wait to hear what happened." They arrived home forty-five minutes later. Hektor took Laura in his arms and held her tightly.

"Thanks again for making my studies and an academic career a reality. And you are right; I've never started anything I haven't finished. This situation won't be an exception. It will take some patience and planning; we'll get there eventually." Laura became concerned.

"Tell me; what went wrong?"

"It's nothing personal; the job opportunities in Germanic literatures and languages seem to be absolutely dismal. There were five times as many PhDs as there were job offers in my discipline. It's obviously not an area with huge demand for people having a terminal degree. I can't wait to talk to Dr. Harcourt about it."

"Well, that does put a damper on things, but let's relax and then discuss how to proceed. Somehow I know you'll come up with the right answers."

"I should have studied Russian or Chinese; that might have been more productive. But I didn't."

"Let's sleep on it and see what happens."

They attended church the next morning. The guest speaker was the principal of the Detroit School for the Deaf. He was looking for some financial support from the congregation. The entire time the man was talking, Hektor's mind was racing. *That's sort of language related; I wonder what kind of degree the guy has?*

As always, Hektor was seated at the end of the pew. The service ended, and Laura was chatting with a few of their friends. She wasn't even aware that Hektor had gotten up and was trying to corner the guest speaker. He caught him as he was ready to leave the church.

"Hi, I'm Hektor Birken. We are members of this church."

"I'm Dan Hollander. Nice to meet you."

"Sir, do you have a few minutes? I'm intrigued by the work you are doing. Would you mind telling me what kind of a degree you have and share a bit about your profession?"

"Oh, not at all. My terminal degree is in audiology. We do some interesting work with deaf children at our school. At one time, I was debating whether I wanted to get my degree in education of the deaf but ultimately wound up at the medical school. It's been a good fit for me. Why are you interested in the school?" Hektor told him about his background and his observations at the MLA conference and his sudden interest in possibly switching tracks. Dr. Hollander gave him sound advice.

"Why don't you plan on visiting our institution for a couple of days? That will give you some firsthand experience in seeing what we do. After that, let's sit down and talk about your options. Could you see me next week?"

"How about Tuesday and Thursday? The other days I have teaching commitments in one of the language departments."

"Tuesday and Thursday work fine for me. How about meeting me at my office at ten o'clock?"

"That's great. I look forward to learning more about your profession."

They shook hands, and Dr. Hollander headed for his car. Just then, Laura spotted Hektor. She had looked everywhere and was beginning to wonder if he had gone to a restroom and perhaps had become ill or something.

"There you are! I was wondering what happened to you. When I looked up, you had disappeared."

"Sorry, I wanted to catch the speaker since I had some questions for him. He's an interesting man. I'm visiting him at the school next week. I'm really curious as to what the whole thing is all about."

"Interesting, interesting!" That was all Laura could say.

"You may think I'm crazy, but to me it feels almost like a calling. I can't wait to learn more about the school and the degree programs he spoke about."

Hektor arrived at the school at the appointed time and was met by Dr. Hollander.

"Let me show you the varying testing facilities and some of our therapy chambers and classrooms. As you can see, we use every possible avenue to communicate with and teach these children; we even resort to the use of sign language but not as extensively as is done at other institutions." The term "sign language" caught Hektor's ear, although the vibes he got were not exactly the most favorable relative to other modes of teaching the children.

"There are two different routes to getting your terminal degree, should you become interested in entering this field of study. You could speak either with Dr. Richardson in the Department of Education of the Deaf and eventually wind up with an EdD or you could meet with Dr. Garrett in the Department of Audiology and get your PhD in that discipline. I chose the latter route and have never been sorry. It's a rigorous program, but you could probably be done in four years. I'd be happy to set up some appointments for you. What do you say?"

"Why don't you make contact with Dr. Richardson in Education of the Deaf first? Somehow, that doesn't sound quite so intimidating. Science has never been my strongest suit."

And so, he met first with Dr. Richardson. Unfortunately, the road laid out by her seemed endlessly long. Having to take numerous "methods courses" would delay a starting point toward the terminal degree by more than two years. That held no appeal to Hektor. He might not start to work and teach until he was forty-three years old, which seemed simply too far into the future. He called Dr. Garrett, who listened intently to Hektor's background and how he had gotten his name.

"I would like to meet with you tomorrow at five thirty, if that is OK with you."

"That sounds great. My last class of teaching in the German Department ends at five o'clock, and I won't have any difficulty getting down to your part of the campus by five thirty."

"Young man, I meant meeting me at five thirty in the morning. I'm usually down here by four thirty; I'm an insomniac. I hope you don't mind getting out of bed early."

"No problem; I'll see you Friday." He almost said "bright eyed and bushy tailed" but caught himself. The clinic was located in one of the "better" neighborhoods in Detroit. All Hektor carried was a low-caliber briefcase. He made it OK to Dr. Garrett's office.

"Come in, come in, young man. Have a seat and let me take a look at your transcripts." It didn't take him all that long.

"Your grades are impressive. You want my honest opinion? This is a very different profession from that in which you are presently immersed. However, looking at what you have done in four years and how well you have done it, I see absolutely no problem with you joining our department. Anyone who obviously reads and writes our language as well as you do must be able to undertake such a major switch in direction and should have no difficulty learning what we teach.

"Here are my suggestions. Keep your teaching contract for the upcoming academic year and take three or four prerequisite classes at your convenience. Our departments operate on totally different campuses, and none of what you are doing can be interpreted as devious. We'll see how well you like our disciplines, and you will discover how well you like us. Fair enough?"

"Sounds interesting to me! I certainly would like to give it a try."

"After you have taken some of the prerequisites, I want to meet with you again and discuss the outcome of your studies. If the results are mutually pleasing, you will start full time with us in fall 1970. You'll have a twenty-hour clinical commitment in various settings aside from your academic studies and receive an annual tax-free research grant of five thousand dollars. Tuition and books are paid for as well. Does any of this appeal to you?"

"That's fair enough to me. Let me share your information with my wife. May I call you on Monday with my decision?" Dr. Garrett peered over his slipping glasses and smiled.

"I look forward to having you in the department, Hektor. Let me walk you to the elevator." They shook hands; both men felt good about their first meeting.

Hektor was glad for the daylight as he was making his way to his car in the parking garage and was pleased to see that the structure was policed twenty-four seven. He couldn't wait to see Laura and called her at the office at GM.

"Dr. Haviland's office, Laura Birken speaking."

"Honey, it's me. Could we meet for lunch? I've got some interesting news to share."

"That sounds exciting. I could use some good news today. Meet me in the lobby. I'll think of a place to grab a bite in the meantime. Ciao! See you at noon." *That sounded like Audrey Hepburn in "Roman Holiday" and not like my Laura.* Not wanting to waste any time, they went to a little coffee shop in the building. They quickly placed their order and sat down.

"Well, tell me. What did Dr. Garrett have to say? What's he like?"

"He's quite the character, but I like him. You know me and liking people who don't beat around the bush. That's Dr. Garrett in a nutshell." He told Laura about their conversation and his recommendations.

"That sounds wonderful. Now, I'm beginning to believe it's a calling. It's just uncanny how this whole thing came about. How do you feel about it?"

"I have nothing to lose but the tuition I will pay for the three or four prerequisite classes I'm taking. If I do well enough and switch to audiology, they'll reimburse me for the cost of taking those classes as well. I'll teach my classes and keep mum in the Department about the new direction I'm taking. I won't have to withdraw from Michigan until the last minute. No harm done all the way around. To tell you the truth, I'm excited about this. If I study hard enough and stick with it, I should have my PhD when I'm forty. That's not too bad."

"You're darn right, it's not too bad." She lifted her ice tea glass toward Hektor. "Here's to you, Dr. Birken. I'm thrilled and will do anything to make this a reality for you. I love you very much!" She took his hands and kissed them.

"I have to run. There are piles and piles of stuff on my desk I need to finish before I leave this afternoon. Pick me up by the side door." She blew him a kiss as she caught the elevator to her floor. Ever since the riots of 1967, Laura liked ducking out the building by the side door rather than the main entrance on Grand Boulevard. Hektor saw her walking out, purse and wig in hands.

"Why aren't you wearing your wig?"

"I couldn't stand it any longer; it felt like I was wearing a girdle on my head. It will go in the trash can when I get home. I'll never wear that thing again even if I have to see Lottie twice a week. That wig is deadly."

"Uh-oh! Things must have gotten hot at the office this afternoon!"

"You aren't just a-kidding. Some of those people can drive me crazy. I'm glad I really like my cohort and my immediate boss. I can't wait to have a glass of wine when I get home. I'm still so excited about the good news you shared at lunchtime. Aren't you thrilled?"

"I am—and overwhelmed. It's all such different stuff. Can you imagine me studying 'Anatomy and Physiology' of anything? The other offerings sound less intimidating, but I will do my best."

He had taken copious notes in his first anatomy class and wasn't sure what it was all about. Even Laura, with her experience as an office assistant in a medical practice, couldn't make heads or tails out of what Hektor had written.

"My problem is, half of the time I have no clue what the guy is mumbling. I wish he'd be more articulate."

"Why don't you ask him if he'd object if you recorded his lectures? We could transcribe the recordings at night. That might help."

Hektor did receive permission to record the anatomy lectures and was amazed at Laura's readings of the text. It made all the difference in the world. He was off and running. Between work and studying, the months flew by quickly. Laura decided to join Hektor when he met with Dr. Garrett to discuss his academic future.

Dr. Garrett took an immediate liking to Laura. Before long, they were talking about cooking and certain favorite recipes. *What about me? What about my academic program?* Of course, there were no problems.

"We look forward to having you in the Department starting in September. I know you'll do well. Be sure to enroll in Dr. Lovell's 'Anatomy and Physiology of the Auditory Mechanism'. It's perfect timing after you did the one on the Speech Mechanism; Dr. Lovell only offers it every other year. This is great. He's a taskmaster, but I'm sure that the two of you will get along fine. He likes nontraditional students; he thinks they are there to learn and not merely to occupy a seat in class." Hektor and Laura knew he had made a sound decision.

"Be sure to come to the cocktail party early in the fall; I want to introduce you to the faculty and have you meet the other new doctoral students entering the program. It will be nice for Laura to know the staff and the spouses of the other students. I'm proud of the camaraderie among our faculty, staff, and students. It's a very special bunch of people." He got out of his chair and gave Laura a hug.

"It's really nice to meet you, young lady. You two will do OK. Don't be a stranger in the department, Laura. I would love to talk to you some more—about things other than this guy's progress." Hektor and Laura were holding hands when they got on the elevator. Dr. Garrett smiled broadly as he walked by his secretaries' desks.

"Nice kids," said he as he knocked on the closest desk and winked at his two favorite gals, Yolanda and Patricia. The next time they all met was at the cocktail party. The departmental reception was an elegant affair with cocktails and lavish hors d'oeuvres served professionally. Dr. Garrett knew how to do a party right. The highlight of the event was meeting Esteban Blanco and his beautiful bride, Irinia. Theirs was a friendship at first sight, a friendship that ultimately would last a lifetime.

⋊⋉

Hektor and Laura kept trying to get pregnant and began to wonder why Laura ever took birth-control pills. Discussing the matter with Dr. Humburg, he suggested they explore the matter with a colleague addressing fertility issues. Both Laura and Hektor went through numerous sessions to ascertain their respective fertility and were subjected to many physical explorations of their reproductive organs. Eventually, it was speculated that malfunctioning of Laura's fallopian tubes prevented them from achieving their goal.

Dr. Humburg began talking about adoption, a choice Laura was willing to consider but not Hektor. He kept hoping that he and Laura would be capable of producing their own offspring. At this point, he was at his wit's end. Going through the gauntlet of fertility testing and ending with the consideration of adoption had been more than painful for both Hektor and Laura.

)(

Hektor liked all of his professors and did very well in most of his classes. His least favorite subjects were statistics and psychoacoustics. He liked the professors who taught the classes; he just didn't care for the information they had to impart. He could have lived without that knowledge, but these minor areas were required and necessary evils. He was lucky to finish with solid B pluses in those nemeses.

His clinical experiences presented with a rough start as well. The assignment almost torpedoed the adventure into his newly chosen field. He had absolutely no respect for the first supervisor with whom he was forced to work. Hektor finally confronted the man and eventually discussed his predicament with his mentor. He finished the three-month-long challenging stint with the understanding he would never again be assigned to the site. Hektor's favorite clinical assignments—and there were many—were his year at Children's Hospital and his turn at Detroit General.

Hektor adored his supervisor at Children's Hospital; she often made him smile. One story he never forgot. She admitted she often drove with too heavy a foot on the gas pedal and was pulled over by a Wayne County sheriff for speeding on the Edsel Ford Expressway. She drove to the side of the road and rolled down the window as the sheriff approached to ask for her license. With the biggest smile she could muster, she looked at the handsome man.

"Oh, officer I know exactly what you are trying to do. You want to sell me more tickets to the policeman's ball."

"Ma'am, Wayne County sheriffs don't have balls!" he sputtered, almost startled by her inquiry. Of course, he realized immediately what he had said. He winked at her and tapped his cap.

"Ma'am, you go easy on the gas and drive more carefully. Have a nice day!" he said as he turned away quickly. She could hear him laughing all the way back to his vehicle.

A few weeks later, she drove through a red light on her way to the hospital. Within seconds she saw the gumball machine behind her. She stepped on the gas and drove at breakneck speed to the closest gas station. Flushed, she headed straight for the john. When she stepped out, the officer who had followed her was waiting for her emergence from the loo.

"Ma'am, do you realize you went through a red light and then tried to avoid me by speeding? I could arrest you and put you in the clink!"

"I know, sir. But you see, I have the shits, and I couldn't afford to soil my panties. I'm on duty at the hospital up the street."

"Well, in that case I will look the other way. I wouldn't want you to work with smelly panties with those poor children. Please be more careful the next time." He commenced with the inimitable heel clicking and marched back to his colleague waiting for the verdict in the patrol car. She couldn't help overhearing him.

"I'll be damned; now I've heard it all!" he said and slammed the car door.

※

By the time 1973 rolled around, Hektor was comfortable in his chosen profession. His favorite teachers in the language department never forgave him for deserting their discipline, but they understood. They were convinced he would have done well staying with his first love.

The Blancos and Birkens weathered many a storm during those four years of intensive training. Irinia and Laura were the most supportive spouses any husband could ever wish for. Both were working gals who were earning their own degrees—PhT (Putting Husband Through). Almost for the entire period, the women took turns preparing spectacular meals on alternating Saturdays entertaining the happy, hard-working foursome. A favorite game was Double Pinochle. All loved the movies and often took advantage of reduced tickets Irinia managed to get somewhere. None of them ever forgot the night they went to see *The Way We Were*. It remained one of their all-time favorites. Laura often reminded Hektor of the magic night after seeing the movie.

"You made love to me three times that night; that never happened before and unfortunately ever again." Approaching his fortieth birthday, Hektor began to seriously doubt the advisability of becoming a father that late in life. He decided to have a vasectomy as soon as the opportunity presented itself.

During the spring and summer of 1973, Esteban and Hektor met regularly every Saturday at the department library in preparation for their doctoral exams. The week of exams came and went. Hektor had received special permission to be sequestered with his IBM Selectric typewriter in a small cubicle. He never could have managed to write all he did by hand. Walking out of his self-imposed cell after forty hours of hammering away, he handed his last pages to the departmental secretary.

"It better be good enough, because I'll never do it a second time!" After letting them sit on hot coals for six weeks, Dr. Garrett called Hektor and Esteban, respectively, for conferences in his office. Dr. G. realized how anxious Hektor obviously was; he was his oldest student among several who sat for the exams.

"Young man, I won't keep you on the hot seat; you passed the exam with flying colors." He shook Hektor's hand; a generous smile crossed his wrinkled face.

"We even passed you in your two 'favorite' minor subjects. My colleagues and I agreed—what you wrote on statistics and psycho-acoustics was a lot of BS, but you wrote it so eloquently, we had no choice but to pass you. You will make a wonderful teacher." He shook Hektor's hand again.

"Go home and celebrate with Laura."

Esteban and Irinia got the good word as well. The happy foursome went to Mario's and had one heck of a celebration. All four had earned it. Of course, now came the final touch: their dissertations and the process of finding jobs.

The dissertation process was at times frustrating and extremely challenging for students and mentor alike. This was one area where Dr. Garrett turned out to be most demanding. Hektor had written the first three chapters of his dissertation when it was time for Dr. G. to head for Madeline Island in Wisconsin for his annual fishing trip.

A week after Dr. Garrett's departure, Hektor found a thick envelope in their mail box. He opened it carefully and discovered the pages of his first three chapters. Most were covered with greasy fingerprints, smelled fishy, and bore hundreds of markings in red ink. In addition, there was a cassette tape. Hektor sat down in their living room and listened to Dr. Garrett's commentary. He was thankful that he was alone in the house. He became madder by the minute and eventually screamed.

"You damn fucking bastard! I expected better!" He was glad that Dr. Garrett could not be reached by phone on Madeline Island. By the time the man had returned rejuvenated to Detroit, Laura had succeeded in calming Hektor sufficiently.

⋈

The almost newly baked doctors interviewed at various places for their first jobs. Esteban wound up at Michigan State, and Hektor eventually accepted a position as Assistant Professor at Hinterland University in Iowa. Laura's mother couldn't understand why Hektor wanted to take a job in *I-O-W-A!* The way Mom said it, you would have thought he planned to transplant them to the moon.

"I'll tell you why Iowa appealed to me. First of all, it's a clinical and teaching situation that suits me and allows me to shape a new program and put my stamp on it. And—I liked waking up to news on future-market prices for pork bellies, fertilizers, corn, and soybeans rather than on how many people had been murdered overnight. It was totally refreshing coming from Detroit. I think we'll learn to appreciate living in the middle of the country with down-to-earth folks."

"Now that you're putting it in those words, I can accept your decision. Personally, I'm a big-city kind of gal. Just don't forget where you came from. I wish you all the luck and happiness in the world."

The guys started working in August while their spouses stayed behind to deal with the selling of homes and preparations for the big move to distant locations. Hektor and Laura counted their blessings; their home sold in late August with a mutually agreeable closing date. All things considered, they were pleased with the final outcome. They didn't make a lot of money and essentially broke even. Hektor had flown to Iowa, leaving the car for Laura to get around. He found a room with an elderly lady near campus. Hektor made the hovel his own; the lady was sweet and super friendly. Dusting was clearly not her forté. The first weekend on board, Hektor took the opportunity to do a major cleanup job while the lady of the house went out for lunch with a group of elderly dames.

He spent his evenings typing, always responding to the latest suggestions and/or corrections arriving almost daily from Detroit. He had taken the position in Hinterland with Dr. Garrett's promise of not letting "out of sight/out of mind" become the operative word with reference to the completion of the dissertation. Dr. G. kept his word—and Laura and Hektor kept busy. Hektor did a lot of writing and rewriting and made the USPS rich with the daily special deliveries traveling between Hinterland and Detroit and vice versa. It was Laura who took on the role of messenger; she got along famously with Dr. G.

Aside from testing the waters of teaching in his new discipline,

Hektor always had his antennas out for finding a house. It was clearly a market with very few desirable homes for sale. When a colleague brought a house on Fourth Street to his attention, he jumped on the opportunity and bought it without even consulting Laura.

Ж

Hektor had his defense in early September. In the end, both Esteban and Hektor survived all the hurdles and passed their final orals. Hektor's had a humorous ending to his final hazing. There was the matter of a last question to be presented.

"What is the difference between a hearing aid and an auditory trainer?"

He gave his inquiring professors a multitude of correct answers only to be asked again and again, "And what else is different?" He finally had enough.

"One gets screwed on the head and the other on a table." His committee cracked up. They knew they had gotten the better of him, having pushed him to his limits.

"Please step out while we discuss your performance," finally announced one of the committee members. It didn't take long before he was called back and told he had passed the last gauntlet. It was all over but the shouting. The happy couple had good reason to rejoice.

Ж

After several temporary housing arrangements in Hinterland, Hektor and Laura moved into their home on Fourth Street in October 1974. Both thought the closing on the deal was a hoot. Hektor inquired if he needed to bring a certified check to finalize the transaction.

"Oh no. Bring your personal checkbook. That will do perfectly."

He couldn't believe what he was hearing. When the dust had settled, Hektor asked about keys for the house.

"Sorry, we have none. We never lock any doors."

That didn't work for anyone who had recently moved from Detroit, Michigan, to Hinterland, Iowa. On their way out of the bank, they found a phone number for a locksmith in the yellow pages. The good man met them promptly at the house. Before they retired that night, they had keys for both front and back doors. These were the kinds of wonderful discoveries they made living in a small and sleepy midwestern town.

Hektor and Laura, especially Laura, met the challenge of updating and renovating a forty-year-old custom-built home with a vengeance. Once the hardwood floors were refinished, tons of paint applied, cupboard doors updated, umpteen rolls of wallpaper professionally hung, and new light fixtures installed, it turned into a pretty nifty place.

The Blancos would nest in Michigan for the next six years and eventually produced three beautiful children. Hektor and Laura were not that lucky; having children was a pleasure that unfortunately eluded them. But they had each other. Eventually, they had six godchildren whose achievements they celebrated with pride.

Their move to Hinterland away from the challenges of Detroit was largely a positive experience. Hektor and Esteban were awarded their PhDs in the field of audiology on December 10, 1974. The long and winding road leading to a life in academia was finally over.

One of Hektor's new colleagues was married to a general surgeon. He didn't know how they got on the subject, but at the first faculty cocktail party he and Laura attended, Hektor asked him if he did something like a vasectomy.

"Sure, no problem. I usually perform them right in our offices; it saves the guy a bundle of money not having to spend two to three days in the hospital. Call our secretary and make an appointment for me to do you. It may be a few weeks before I can get to you. Cheers! Nothing to it!"

Ouch! But he would deal with it. Three weeks later he was on the operating table having his "little, nothing-to-it" procedure. Once the anesthesia wore off, he was one very sore puppy for about a week. He would have preferred to stand under a hot shower, followed by ice packs bracing his "family jewels," instead of sitting in a chair grading papers, doing lesson plans, or testing patients' hearing. He survived and in the end was satisfied to know that there would be no unwanted pregnancies in the future.

Chapter 3

HEKTOR'S office at the university at last had become livable during the Christmas break. All of his books were unpacked and stashed away properly; paintings and diplomas were hung. Recycled draperies and an old rug warmed up the otherwise sterile room; Hektor was convinced he had arrived. He needed his office to have a homey atmosphere since he anticipated being seriously engrossed in his work for many hours each day.

The reality of functioning in the real world began to sink in. Hektor had been too busy for the past nine years working toward his professional goals to think about what he had given up. Suddenly, a multitude of questions floated through his mind. *Were our sacrifices too great? Did I miss opportunities to earn heaps of money and a comfortable life for the sake of earning a PhD?*

Lately he was beginning to reflect on his age. He had lived for twenty years in the United States. *What do I have to show for this time by comparison to other men my age? Did I fritter away the most productive years in most men's lives in order to achieve what I should have accomplished at a much-younger age? Even in our marital bed, I've been a failure. Why didn't we have at least one child of our own? Laura would have been a wonderful mother.*

He looked at himself as having reached the midpoint of his life.

While he was glad there wouldn't be any surprise bundles of joy at this stage, he still felt utterly disappointed that it hadn't happened when they were younger, knowing how much Laura would have loved to have his child.

On one of those mornings in early 1975, he faced his image in the mirror as he was shaving a day's growth of stubble. He didn't like what he saw. He ran his hands through his hair. *What's happening to me? My God, my temples are turning gray. I don't think I will ever get used to these bifocals.* He thought his face was pudgy, showing signs of overweight. Never mind his face; his whole body had gone to pot. Peggy Lee's 1969 hit "Is That All There Is?" rang in his ears.

He didn't realize it then, but on that auspicious morning, he opened Pandora's Box. His actions would bring Laura and him to an abyss of emotional trauma neither one of them thought their relationship could survive. Both of them faced a reality that would test their love for each other to a degree neither of them imagined was possible. Hektor's behavior would create for Laura a hell on earth during the next twelve months.

In March, both he and Laura had the shock of their lives. Helena and Alex Birken announced they would arrive in Chicago by "yumbo yet" in early May.

"I didn't know they built a bridge across the Atlantic," was Hektor's pronouncement after he finished reading his mother's letter.

"She always said that would be the only way she would visit us in America. Perhaps curiosity got the better of her? I believe she finally accepted the fact I am settled in this country and will never return to Germany permanently. And don't forget, it has been eight years since we visited them last. Perchance, absence has made the heart grow fonder?" Laura was thrilled to know that her in-laws were willing to make the journey.

"Whatever their reasons, I am excited about their coming to be with us. It will be good for them to see for themselves where and how we live, where you work, and to meet some of our friends. There is nothing like seeing things through your own eyes and to actually experience a place. Pictures are great, but they are no substitute for the true enjoyment of the encounter." Hektor agreed with Laura's assessment. He kept reading and rereading his mother's letter.

"I still haven't figured out what prompted them to make this journey. Was it sheer inquisitiveness? Whatever the reason, it's one of the wisest investments they will make in time and money. I only wish they had done it sooner. Mother has been suffering and dealing with my leaving Germany for a long twenty-one years. She keeps reminding me that she still can see that hateful vessel taking me away into the New World."

Before they departed for O'Hare Airport, Hektor received a phone call from his long-standing friends, Else and Walter Gunders. They were venturing on another cross-country trip of the States. After sampling the East Coast, they would arrive in Chicago, visiting some friends dating back to their youth. The upshot of the phone call was an arrangement convenient for Hektor and Laura. The day they would take Hektor's parents back to O'Hare, they would pick up Walter and Else for a three-week visit to Hinterland.

Anyone would have thought that six weeks of house guests would be a challenge to any marriage. Hektor and Laura didn't mind; they knew Walter and Else would be easier to have than Hektor's parents.

At last, the day of his parent's arrival was at hand. Hektor took his binoculars with him, making it easier to spot Helena and Alex as they emerged from one of the exits of the Boeing 747. He had no difficulty recognizing his folks. Helena was wearing a pale green suit and carrying her typical oversized handbag. His father, still a very large man, was sporting one of his caps, a style Hektor never would have worn as a younger man.

The plane was filled to capacity, making the retrieval of luggage and passing INS and Customs a lengthy process. When it was time for greetings and hugs, Helena resembled a hen ready to breed her next brood of chickens. Her face was as red as a beet, and she kept huffing and puffing. Having survived the first leg of the adventure of a lifetime, she had difficulty breathing the heavy, humid midwestern air.

"*Heiss, viel zu heiss!*" [Hot, much too hot!] was her first utterance before she said "hello."

"Let me go and get our car. It has climate control." He left Laura to fend for herself. At least they were not total strangers. Initially, the air conditioning was a welcome change. By the time they stopped on the outskirts of Chicago for a bite to eat, his parents had cooled off sufficiently and started to complain about it being too drafty.

"The cool air in the car is blowing on our heads. We will probably come down with neuralgia. You know I never could tolerate cross ventilation," Helena reminded her son. How well he could remember the circus he lived through all of his days in Germany.

"Please, please, no draft. I'll become deathly ill." Hektor couldn't remember how often he had heard people use that inane phrase. He learned to appreciate the welcome relief from cross ventilation his first night in the United States. Rather than fighting with his parents shortly after their arrival, he switched the car to vent. He knew they would be asking him to turn the AC back on sooner or later. And he was right.

The six-hour drive to Hinterland after the transatlantic flight just about did his folks in. When Hektor pulled into the drive at Fourth

Street, Helena and Alex Birken were carrying on a loudness contest in snoring. Hektor and Laura brought in their luggage and soon had them lying in their comfortable beds. There would be plenty of time the next day to explore, comment on, and criticize and/or praise the home of their son and daughter-in-law.

The family reunion was not all milk and honey. German people can be terribly critical of other people's customs. But on the whole, the visit to "America" was a success. The firsthand experience of seeing Hektor and Laura in their home in a pleasant environment, meeting their friends, and watching their son at work created a very real picture of the prodigal son now established in "that" foreign and damnable land.

One thing was certain: Helena gained a totally different impression of Laura's lifestyle in Hinterland. The advent of television and watching American movies had given Hektor's mother the idea that most American women were flitting around their homes in fancy negligés and talking on color-coordinated telephones as they moved from room to room in their fancy modern homes. They were pampered creatures who were more concerned about the color or shape of their finger- and toenails than anything else. The reality hit home when Helena observed Laura running and keeping a large home and doing her own cooking and bread baking, while maintaining a responsible part-time position in city government. This reality check gave Helena a totally new appreciation of her American daughter-in-law.

One of the highlights of his parents' vacation in Hinterland was the first visit to Hektor's office. Recalling the event, Hektor can still see his mother standing in his office, gently and lovingly running her right hand over his doctoral diploma. Hektor looked at his mother.

"What's wrong, Mutti? Why are you crying?" She turned around to face him.

"I am so proud of you. To think what you have achieved. I am seeing my own dreams realized through you. Contrary to what I wrote to you nine years ago, you did the right thing by following your dream. Thank you, Hektor! You have earned the station in life where you are. It was a long, long road, a long, long battle!"

"You are right, Mother. It was a long road and not always an easy one. Now that I'm at this point in my life, I'm no longer so sure it was all worth it. I wonder if the price that we paid was perhaps too high. Oh, I love my work and what we have achieved but also think of all the wealth we might have accumulated had I stayed in business for all those years instead of sitting on school benches to earn this diploma. Maybe you were right when you told me I was crazy to give up all those wonderful opportunities that once were dangled in front of my eyes."

"Son, you are wrong. Money isn't everything. I made a mistake trying to discourage you from pursuing your dreams. I never was allowed to follow mine. I can't tell you how pleased I am with both of you, and especially Laura, for making it possible for you to realize yours."

"It makes me smile, Mother, to hear you say 'money isn't everything.' I never thought I would hear you say those words. Money was always so important to you and to everyone in your family. The concept was drilled into you from the time you were old enough to understand what it was all about. It must be true that we become wiser with age.

"Perhaps you are right. But look at me; I'm not a young man any longer. More than half of my life is gone. What do I have to show for it? Yes, we have a nice home and lovely things. I have a respectable job and enjoy what I'm doing. What really hit me were the rewards I earned after studying for eight years. Laura earned more money as a secretary without any kind of a degree. My starting salary in academia was less than seventy percent of what I earned nine years earlier. How do you think that made me feel? I sure didn't feel like a winner."

"I'm sorry you see it that way. I thought you would be happy with what both of you have achieved. Perhaps, in time you will view things in a more positive light. The passing of years will do that for you." She put her arms around Hektor and hugged him firmly. There were still tears flooding her eyes.

Hektor truly believed that his parents, especially his mother, always harbored the hope of his permanent return to the family fold in Germany. Visiting them in Hinterland allowed his parents to reach closure and acceptance in a grieving process that had lasted far too long.

Helena was truly impressed with all that Hektor had accomplished. His father loved what Hektor was doing with little deaf children. He was so happy for him that he found his niche in life at last, be it ever so far away from his family. Alex thought his son was content with his life. That allowed him to accept the New World his son had chosen, and he was happy for him.

Hektor was grateful that at least his father thought he was satisfied with his life. After his long talk with his mother, she knew that Hektor sensed there was something missing. Deep down in his heart, he was aware of the performance he was putting on for them. The truth was, he had to face his own demons every morning as he tried to convince himself he indeed had every reason to be content. But he wasn't. He believed his life to be humdrum and boring. He deeply felt, somewhere in his years of living, life had passed him by. He was beginning to believe he should consider analysis.

There was his strange upbringing by a mother who viewed sex as dirty and an obligation rather than a natural and healthy aspect in a good relationship. The sexual encounters with Lothar Zend when he was only eleven years old, the broken engagement with Doretta, his disastrous first marriage with Georgia, and the detachment from his children kept haunting him. Hektor's kinship with Laura was joyful and mutually satisfactory. And yes, he was disappointed that they had not succeeded in having their own children. He envied Esteban and Irinia. He should have been happy with all that he had and all they achieved. *Am I yearning for the kind of relationship I had with Sheila?*

The sexual revolution of the sixties and seventies entered into the picture. Anything one wanted to see was readily depicted in word and picture and available in every inner city and on the internet. It was the bottom of the pool of curiosity to which Hektor began to be drawn. *Is contentment and humdrum existence really all there will be for the remainder of my days?* He was clearly experiencing a crisis and was willing to test the waters of wantonness.

Laura had to be out of town due to a death in the family. She made an emergency trip south. Hektor was left for a few days to fend for himself with his parents. It worked out OK. His father's incessant smoking in the air-conditioned house finally got to Hektor. He knew first hand, no one has a worse attitude toward smokers than a reformed smoker. He had to get out of the house. No way was he becoming reacquainted with that evil addiction.

⚹

His very last patient at WSU had taught him a lesson. Half of her face had been cut away. He was to assess her bone conduction function. Bending over her, she could see the pack of cigarettes in the pocket of his white shirt. She gestured for pen and paper and wrote.

"Take a good look at me. It's from those damn things that I got this reward." She pointed at her mutilated face. He had seen the lungs of smokers preserved in formaldehyde and other devastating evidence of what smoking can do to one's body in various labs. None of that hit him as hard as seeing this terribly disfigured face on the woman staring at him. As he walked out of the clinic that night, he reached as usual for his first cigarette. Before he grasped for his lighter, he contemplated the cigarette and spoke out loud.

"You will not be controlled by this little bit of shitty tobacco. You are a smart man. So just put the damn thing back in the box and never touch another cigarette."

He carried the same pack in his shirt for six months. One day he threw it in a public trash can and never had another cigarette or any other smoking device after his encounter with the ill-fated patient. She had indeed taught him a great lesson.

Is it time to deal with my current addiction in a rational manner as I dealt with the addiction to nicotine? He learned of a group of persons who regularly met for the purpose of enjoying each other. Laura's trip south gave him a perfect opportunity to sample the forbidden fruit. Mom and Dad were perfectly happy to be alone for an evening, being able to freely talk German and digesting their American experiences on their own terms. They did not miss Hektor, and Hektor did not miss them. Having taken the first step on the slippery path of pro-miscuity, he acted like a bitch in heat, looking for every possible encounter.

On the other hand, he could not jump over his own shadow of propriety. His conscience was beginning to plague him. *What if Laura finds out? What if my colleagues discover what I am doing? Will everything go down the drain? Is a double life really worth jeopardizing everything we struggled for in the past twelve years? Am I dealing with a mid-life crisis, to resort to a cliché? Is this a delayed seven-year itch? Am I doing to Laura what Georgia did to me? Wake up you damn fool; you are about to piss your life away!*

Hektor had a hard time dealing with his emotional and deep-seated psychological turmoil. His problems were not solved by the presence of his parents. He was fully aware of their unholy matrimonial relationship and the hell they had created for each other over so many years. Adding to his miserable state of mind was a revelation his mother made two nights after Laura's departure for Kentucky.

"I presume you have not been in touch with any of the Osram family?"

"No, Mother, I've never had any contact with Doretta's family after I broke our engagement, and the last time I saw Doretta was during my visit in Zurich in 1963. I knew she and her intended husband were moving to Santiago, Chile, after their child was born in Switzerland. I never heard another word from her. I often wondered what happened to Doretta and Fernando."

"Doretta's mother called me just a few weeks ago. She was sobbing while she was speaking to me on the phone. She told me that a German lady, who had gotten to know Doretta in Santiago, wrote to her after the first of the year.

"Fernando and Doretta were married after their arrival in Chile. The first child was a little boy who was born while they were still in Zurich. Two years later, Doretta gave birth to a little girl in Santiago. Apparently Fernando's family learned to love Doretta and the two beautiful grandchildren she had brought into their lives. Doretta at last found happiness and contentment in the New World.

"I'm so sorry to share this with you, but the woman wrote that Doretta, their children, and Fernando and his entire family disappeared after the Pinochet coup d'état on September 11, 1973. None of them were ever heard from again. She presumed that they were all executed subsequent to that infamous day as were so many others." Hektor was stunned.

"No, I have not heard anything about Doretta and what might have happened. Needless to say, after we parted in Zurich twelve years ago, neither one of us made any further attempts at getting in touch. We believed it wasn't the thing to do in view of Doretta and Fernando's troubled return to Chile and his family's attitude toward Doretta to begin with. Furthermore, Laura and I met shortly after my return from Europe, and we were married six months later. Laura had enough dealing with a former wife and two children, never mind a former fiancée. Tragic! I never would have thought that our splitting up would take her down such a devastating road. I'm shocked!"

He went to the bar and poured himself a double scotch—and it wasn't diluted with milk! He couldn't help thinking of Harry. Right now he needed to be alone with his thoughts. Somehow he couldn't deal with his mother's droning and lecturing him on what he did to that poor girl. He didn't need her to lay that trip on him again and again.

Looking back on his parents' visit, one of the saddest moments occurred a day or two before their return to Germany. Laura and Helena were shopping or visiting friends. Hektor and his father were sitting in the living room having a friendly discussion. They were talking around or through a giant bouquet of lilacs placed on a table between them; the fragrance was overpowering. Hektor's father looked at him with those big brown and very sad eyes.

"Your mother never forgave you for leaving Germany. She finally seems to have come to terms with your living in this country. She told me about your discussion with her a few days ago. Your mother is right; she has finally learned that money isn't everything. You ought to be happy with what you and Laura have achieved."

"Dad, I am happy in many ways, and I am thankful for the station in life I've attained. I suppose I can't have everything my way."

"I'm glad you have found happiness in this foreign land."

What a joke!

Alex continued.

"I dislike not being able to speak English with other people or not to understand what people are saying about anything. The language barrier bothers me immensely. I'm always glad when it is only us, and we can return to speaking German. Laura is trying very hard to improve her German, and Mother and I truly appreciate her wishing to communicate with us. You should be making a greater effort and speak German with her more often. She told me you are not very good about doing it. She certainly tries, and we are pleased with all she does, grammatical errors and all."

"Well, Dad, I'm happy we had this chance to talk—just you and I. We haven't done it in years. I always remembered and treasured the times when you first got me interested in opera and we could talk about different singers and identify famous arias. I will be forever thankful for the love of classical music, especially opera, you instilled in me when I was very young."

Hektor didn't realize it at that moment, but it was to be the last conversation he would have with his father. He remembered sitting there, making idle conversation, almost choking on the tears he feared to show. What he really wanted to do was to put his arms around his dad and thank him for his legacy, for all he allowed him to be. He wanted to tell him how much he really loved him, but he didn't. He let the opportunity pass.

Hektor's heart was filled with sadness as they made the long drive back to Chicago. His Dad liked the stopover in Dubuque. Standing by the Mississippi, he quietly hummed "Ole Man River," his voice barely echoing the rich baritone quality it once had.

"You don't sing much anymore, Dad, do you? I thought you liked the men's chorus. You don't go any longer? That was such a great way for you to do something you truly enjoyed."

"I did, but my voice isn't what it used to be, and Mother didn't like to be alone at home for long evenings, especially during the winter months. So, I gave it up, or should I say, it gave me up?"

They had their picture taken with the skyscrapers of Chicago and posed in front of the much-feared "Yumbo Yet." The adventure of a lifetime almost had come full circle. All had to be "strong" for their goodbyes and not shed any tears in front of strangers. Both Laura and Hektor hugged both of them as they were getting ready to board the plane. Hektor finally uttered his last words.

"You be safe and have a good flight. It was wonderful having you with us. Thank you for coming to see Laura and me in our new home. See you soon!" They were off. Hektor was relieved that the visit had been largely a positive experience all around.

The plane carrying Hektor's parents disappeared in the clouds. He was strong and did not shed any tears—then. They had been shed invisibly and inside on that afternoon when the heady fragrance of freshly cut lilacs hung in the air of the living room in Hinterland.

Hektor's father died suddenly two years later. Hektor was spared the agony of seeing his dead father. *Or did I deprive myself of dealing with my father's death?* When he finally stood at his graveside, his father was gone for more than a year.

⋊⋉

The departure of his parents was a mixed blessing. On one hand, Hektor was saddened by their leaving; on the other, he was glad they survived the visit without major confrontations. Considering his state of mind, they were a diversion and an indirect protection. Their presence temporarily shielded him from causing greater harm to his relationship with Laura.

Walter and Else's arrival on the scene was a much-needed breath of fresh air. With their worldly and positive approach to life, the Gunders were a welcome change. Laura had absolutely no inkling of the emotional abyss to which Hektor was descending. They spent a relaxing day in Chicago in the company of German friends and made plans for Walter and Else's visit during the subsequent three weeks. When they arrived at the house in Hinterland, Else commented on their trip.

"We really enjoyed the drive from Chicago. We can't get over the abundance of agriculture as soon as we got to the outskirts of the big city. Your college town is charming. We like what you have done with your home. We look forward to visiting Minneapolis and St. Paul. Is there any special place you would care to dine?"

"There is a great restaurant in the North Star Hotel. I'm sure you would enjoy it." They went and were wined and dined in style. It was a splendid evening.

This is exactly what we had in mind," said Else.

"If you don't mind, we would like to return tomorrow night. How about making a reservation for seven o'clock?" Hektor and Laura had no problem with eating at the same restaurant two evenings in a row. It was a real treat since their small town did not offer many outstanding choices of restaurants.

They returned to Iowa after a fun-filled visit to Minneapolis. A few days later, Laura whisked them away on a two-week journey that would take them through Wisconsin and Minnesota, along Lake Superior's north shore and to the western part of Michigan, finishing with a crossing of Lake Michigan by ferry. Hektor flew to Chicago compliments of Else and Walter.

Hektor's reunion with Laura at least temporarily put an end to his shameless conduct. His conscience was nagging at him. Laura was anxious to talk to him since she truly missed him during their two-week separation.

"How are things at home? Did you see anyone? Did some of your colleagues have you over for dinner? How is the summer semester going?"

"There's nothing new at home" He lied by saying he did not see anyone. None of his colleagues saw a need to invite him since he supposedly was busy. The summer semester was going well so far. There were a few more attempts at idle chitchat. The long journey was spent in deafening silence. Laura felt something was bothering her husband, but she had absolutely no idea what could be wrong.

Hektor had started to grow a full beard, decided to shed any extra pounds, and spent much time exercising and getting in shape.

As soon as summer school ended, they drove to Detroit. Laura's father had to be institutionalized. The effects of Alzheimer's on his behavior had become so great that her mother could no longer handle him at home. Witnessing the dreadful aspects of the debilitating disease made Hektor confront his own emotional hell. On one of their last days taking care of Dad, Laura's father had soiled himself for the third or fourth time. Laura stripped him and the bed. Hektor couldn't help watching his young wife washing the body of her emaciated-looking father. Melvin's looks reminded Hektor of images he had seen of concentration camp victims when they were liberated in 1945.

"If I ever learn that I am afflicted with one of these damnable diseases like Alzheimer's, ALS, or Parkinson's, or whatever, I'll kill myself while I can. I hope to God you will never have to do anything like that for me. I'll go for a long walk on a dark and bitter cold night. The Natives have the right idea." Laura put clean pajamas on her dad and tucked him back in bed.

"Please don't even talk like that. It's bad enough your mother always talks about doing herself in. And furthermore, by the time you found out you had one of these problems, it would probably be too late for you to do such a thing. You certainly would not expect me to help you, would you?"

"Sure! I might even buy you a shotgun. That would be quick and efficient."

"No way! I wouldn't want to spend the rest of my days in prison." Hektor decided to let it go. He had other and more pressing issues on his mind.

Hektor drove most of the way from Detroit to Hinterland. They hardly spoke a word. Laura was deep into a book, and when she wasn't reading, she was concentrating on her counted cross stitching. Laura didn't need to be exposed to further trauma, but he was determined to face the music and share his deep, dark secrets with her later. For now, they were looking forward to returning to what had always been their tranquility base, their own home. After making love to Laura, he could no longer continue his deceptions and lies.

"You probably have wondered since our return trip from Chicago what's wrong with me. I am sick. Not physically sick, but emotionally and psychologically. I was a real bastard. Whenever possible, I had a number of illicit encounters. I am still very much in love with you, but I have this primeval urge for which I have no explanation. I'm driven like a bitch in heat." *I'm beginning to hate that phrase!*

Laura went into absolute shock. This was the very last thing she had suspected. She viewed their relationship as sanguine and harmonious, never believing anything was wrong. Laura backed away and glared at Hektor in disgust. She jumped out of bed, not wanting to be anywhere near him.

"Did I understand correctly what you just told me? How long has this been going on?"

"My feelings of having missed out on something and being disenchanted with my life started shortly after I was settled in my office. It all seemed so humdrum. I was wondering if all our sacrifices were for naught."

"How could you do this to me and to us? Why haven't you discussed this with me before?"

Hektor confessed his feelings about himself and the sudden realization that perhaps this was all there was going to be. He believed he had missed much excitement in his life. The latter was far from the truth; perhaps it was the kind of excitement he sought in the darkest spaces of his mind. Shock gave way to anger, and anger gave way to dealing with the problem at hand.

"If you think I will let the last twelve years go down the tubes just like that, you have another thing coming. I love you, and we will work at getting this wreck of a train back on track. If you think I will relinquish you easily, you have to reckon with my German-Irish heritage. If you indeed decide to bring our relationship to a conclusion, it will cost you dearly. In the meantime, the first thing I will do is to finish my own education. Is this the payoff I get for putting you through school for eight long years?" Hektor began to sob.

"I feel like an absolute heel. I'm glad I didn't take Mom up on her offer to take the pistol she always kept under her bed. Of course, I would first have to learn how to use it."

"Please, I don't even want to hear that. I don't know how at this very moment, but somehow we will get through this unholy mess—somehow for sure!"

The remaining months of the year 1975 were pure hell for both. Laura hated the thought of the upcoming holidays. She hated the house where their marriage apparently went on the rocks. Hektor was her rock, but the rock had begun to crumble. Suddenly, she felt adrift.

Chapter 4

THEY made it through the holidays. Shortly after the beginning of the winter semester, Hektor picked up a *Ski* magazine that a client of the clinic had left on the rack in the public area. Reading about various resorts in Colorado and Utah, Hektor was taken back to happier days when he first learned to ski in Oberstdorf in 1953. *I wonder how Laura would feel about taking a real vacation from it all during the coming spring break? Might she be willing to discover the magic of skiing? She's always been athletic. She was an excellent swimmer; she loved water skiing. Why wouldn't she like to discover the wonder of snow skiing?*

He stuck the magazine in his briefcase and broached the subject after dinner that night. Unintentionally, he slapped the magazine on the table. Laura jumped and took one look at the publication so carelessly tossed at her.

"What now? What do you have in mind? I don't like the way you put down that magazine. You've got more bad news for me?" He smiled at her.

"I think we need to put us first for a change. You and I deserve a real vacation and to do something completely new, exciting, and frivolous as you might say. Let's get away from it all. How about if we study some of these advertisements and commit ourselves to a ski vacation during spring break." Laura liked the idea. It sounded frivolous indeed. But they needed frivolous and a spark in their relationship. Hektor was pleased to see Laura smile.

"How about calling this lodge in Vail?" She dialed the number and wasn't too impressed with the responses she received. Perhaps folks from Iowa were not what they were looking for. Hektor flipped through the advertisements of the magazine.

"Try this hotel in Breckenridge; that's somewhat closer to Denver." She called the place and hung up a few seconds later.

"Guess they have bigger fish to fry as well. Why are these people so snooty on the phone? They ought to take courses in public relations. Business must really be booming for these contact persons to be so nonchalant about getting new visitors." Hektor almost gave up. Then he spotted the name of a town he had never heard of before.

"Honey, let me try this one. It's the Visions Lodge & Ski Shoppe in Hideaway Park. I've got no clue where this place is. Supposedly, they are only 65 miles from the Stapleton Airport in Denver." He dialed the number and got a friendly voice at last.

"Our lodge was recently completely renovated. We are only a few minutes from the Winter Park Ski Area. Have you heard of the Mary Jane? It's the newest addition to the ski area. We think you will enjoy your stay with us and fall in love with Hideaway Park." He had gotten the rates for a "quiet, charming room" and was assured it was available for the desired week in March.

"Let me confer with my wife. We'll call you right back to confirm the arrangements. Thank you; you were most helpful." Hektor replaced the receiver and looked at Laura.

"I think this is just what we wanted. We don't need to search any further. It sounds perfect to me. I like the name of the town, and the description of the ski area makes it even more enticing. It's a lot more reasonable than Vail or Breckenridge. Who do we need to impress? Let's do it!"

"You're the boss. If you want to spend money on a vacation, I'm all for it. Lord knows, we do need it. Go ahead and make the reservation, or would you like me to do it?" Laura took over and confirmed the reservation with the Visions Lodge. Next, she managed to order plane tickets for the desired dates. They were all set.

Eventually, they started taking ski lessons at a local park near Hinterland. Maneuvering icy slopes with loaner boots and skis was not exactly the ideal initiation to downhill skiing for Laura. Hektor wasn't much better off. It had been twenty-three years since he stood on skis the first time. But they tried and had a lot of laughs. One time, both of them landed on their butts, tangled up in skis and poles, having stood completely still at the bottom of the bunny hill. Next, they shopped for appropriate clothes; it was a good time to buy them since it was the end of ski season in the Midwest.

Before long, the Ozark DC-9 took off for Stapleton International Airport. They would catch the bus to Hideaway Park and arrive at the lodge in good time. As the bus pulled away from the curb at the airport, Hektor stared out through the smudged windows and looked at the distant mountains.

"I can't believe this. People are golfing and running around in shorts and short-sleeve shirts. I thought the weatherman talked about a recent snowstorm in Denver. This doesn't look anything like what I expected." Laura agreed and sounded alarmed as she spoke hesitantly.

"You think we made a mistake coming this way for spring break? I came prepared to ski, not to hit golf balls."

When the bus pulled off I-70, they noticed huge piles of dirty snow along the road leading to Berthoud Pass. As the bus made the last hairpin turn on the western slope, they marveled at the tall lodge pole pines heavily mantled in blankets of fresh powdery snow. They saw the Visions Lodge shortly after passing Beaver's, only a short walk from where the bus driver dropped them off.

"We are here. This is it. Just look at all that gorgeous white stuff on those roofs. I haven't seen this much snow in years," said Hektor.

They were shown to their room, looking out at old cabins sitting in a splendor of pristine whiteness. They closed the door and contemplated the inviting, comfortable bed. It was the start of a beautiful vacation, the beginning of what they subsequently referred to as "treasured times."

The first day of taking skiing lessons proved what Hektor had predicted. They had to demonstrate their agility and physical readiness to their teacher by crossing one hundred yards on a relatively flat surface with these "new things" strapped to their feet.

"Do it as fast as you can, and try not to land on your butts," was the instructor's advice. Not only did Laura do very well but she actually beat Hektor in the speed contest. They were happy that both qualified to get into the same group. *Wouldn't that have been the pits had we landed in different groups or classes?* Ultimately, Laura became a far better skier than Hektor ever was. Of course, she was almost ten years younger and more daring.

They had seven glorious days with a few inches of fresh snow every night; the days were blessed with sunshine and azure blue skies. The people they met, the classes they took, and the restaurants they sampled all added up to a perfect week. It was almost uncanny. Sometimes, as they rode one of the lifts, they would wonder.

"Is this really happening to us?"

They fell in love all over again; Laura and Hektor discovered they still liked and loved each other very much. The last year flashed before Hektor's eyes. He was sure they had been born again like the Phoenix. He almost destroyed his and Laura's lives; but like the mythical bird, they had risen from their ashes. They found another chance at leading a joyful life.

Emerging from the Ozark DC-9 in Hinterland, Hektor and Laura were suntanned and refreshed. They knew this was not their last ski trip to Colorado. Hektor glanced through the mail and noticed an invitation to a professional meeting to be held in Hideaway Park in early June. He remembered seeing the High Mountain Inn. It was the venue of the prospective meeting.

"You won't believe this, Laura. ARA is having their Summer Institute in Hideaway Park this year. I think I'll plan to attend this one. It will give me an opportunity to see what the village looks and feels like in June." What they didn't realize at that very moment was that Hideaway Park would become one of their favorite venues on earth.

Chapter 5

First thing Monday morning, Hektor completed his absence request to attend the 1976 ARA Summer Institute held in Hideaway Park. The department head approved his projected trip and asked Jolene, his secretary, to book the flight to Denver.

Before Laura and Hektor left for spring break in the Rockies, they learned from Elaine and Charles that his company was moving them to Minneapolis. These were exciting times for Laura; she was so thrilled to have family live closer to her. Having Elaine and Charles and their delightful children, Monty and Margo, only a four-hour drive away from Hinterland was a mighty boost to her morale.

Hektor went to the conference in Colorado. While he was gone, Laura opted to do spring cleaning in preparation for her sister's first visit to Iowa. What she really wanted was a complete change in her appearance. After the ski trip, she thought a more casual hairdo was desirable and would be more practical than the bouffant style she wore throughout her career at GM. She hadn't discussed any details of her plans with Hektor.

Hektor enjoyed the early meetings and chatting with professional colleagues. Dinner at the lodge was a treat. He opted to turn in relatively early. Before he retired, he wanted to make one call.

"Hi, Nora, it's Hektor Birken. My wife and I stayed with you a few months ago. I'm at the High Mountain Inn for a professional meeting."

"Hi. How nice of you to call. Perhaps we can get together while you are here?"

"I'll be free on Wednesday afternoon. If you have a couple of hours, I would love to see what real estate might be available and to our liking. Would you mind showing me around a bit?"

"Not at all. How would it be if I pick you up at two o'clock? I look forward to seeing you again."

Hektor didn't divulge his plans for the afternoon to anyone. If anything came of it, there was always plenty of time for sharing later. Nora met him promptly. They looked at various developments close to town and eventually headed to the neighboring town, Fraser.

The road wound up a hill, and they arrived at Meadow Ridge Condominiums. The complex was developed around a large open meadow never to be built upon. The next buildings to be constructed were units 18A and B along East Meadow Mile. It was a glorious day in the Fraser Valley; the vistas in all directions were spectacular. Hektor brought his Leica along and snapped all sorts of photos. He definitely wanted to know more about these condos under construction. They went to the sales office in Building 7 on West Meadow Mile.

"We expect the next two buildings to be ready for occupancy by Thanksgiving. Unit 18A-1 was sold to a physician, but Unit 2 is still available. It has a most attractive view. Would you care to stand on the approximate spot of its location? I can take you over there; you'll get a pretty good feel for the layout and the views just by standing there." Walking across the meadow, they soon arrived at the site of the future Unit 2. It gave Hektor a fantastic view of Byers Peak with nothing but open land in front of him.

"Are you sure no one will be allowed to build on the meadow or the ridge?"

"I assure you, it is so; it's in the covenants!"

"I would like to buy unit 2. Of course, my wife isn't with me. I want to surprise her. What do I need to do? If I remember correctly, one has ten days to back out of a deal like this, right?"

"Yes, it's right here in your purchase agreement. I will need one thousand dollars in earnest money." Hektor pulled out his checkbook and wrote the check. The salesman prepared the contract. Hektor had done it and almost couldn't believe it was for real.

"Congratulations on your purchase; I don't think you will ever regret having invested in Colorado." As they walked back to the car, Nora just laughed out loud.

"You are really something. How do you think Laura will feel about this? I'm not sure I would have approved of Larry pulling a stunt like that on me. Actually, I think it is a very wise investment. The way things are moving in the valley right now, you will never lose money. It can go only one way, and that is up. Give me a quick call after you get home. I'll be dying to learn how Laura handled your surprise." He stopped at the Visions for a drink before Larry took him back to the High Mountain Inn.

Before he retired that evening, Hektor opened his wallet. He grasped his talisman and held the silver Madonna in his open hands. He asked for her blessings on their future. He called Laura to see how things were in Hinterland, never breathing a word about the purchase of the Birken Hideaway to be built that summer. Things were copacetic on Fourth Street.

"I have been tearing the house apart, doing a major cleaning. It really wasn't all that dirty, but I had this urge to have everything spic and span. You know, it's a woman's thing. Your mother probably would have accused me of having a *Putzfimmel* [rage for cleaning]. Hope you have a great time. I miss you and look forward to seeing you Friday night."

"You wouldn't believe all the snow still on the runs at the ski area. Also, a bunch of us went on a four-wheel drive up to Corona Pass. It was like an arctic wilderness with nothing but snow and ice everywhere. I understand they have ski races up that way on July Fourth every year."

"Sounds like you have renewed your love affair with the mountains. I know how you feel about being in the Rockies. I can hear the joy in your voice. Who knows, maybe someday you will take a position in Colorado. That way you could be closer to 'them thar hills.' Have fun and enjoy it while you are in God's country. Love you, Kirski. Have a safe trip home." (Laura called Hektor "Kirski" jokingly and lovingly after she learned of Helena's dislike of "polish-sounding" names.)

It was hard not to breathe a word about buying the condo. Hektor bit his tongue. He had to be with his wife and see her face when he revealed the surprise upon his arrival in Hinterland.

Soon enough, he would have that pleasure. The DC-9 touched down in the town neighboring Hinterland; Hektor could hardly wait to see Laura. There was something to be said for the small municipal airports of the 1970s—good service and no long waiting in lines.

Laura stood by the outside gate as Hektor scrambled down the steps from the plane. *Why is she wearing a babushka? It must be because of the fresh breeze blowing at the airport.* As Hektor walked up to her, ready to give her a kiss, she yanked off the cover.

"Surprise!" She had turned into a platinum blonde with extremely short-cropped hair. She looked like a regular pixy.

"You like it? It's a little shorter than I thought they would cut it. But you know my hair; it grows so fast."

"I like it. It's really cute and so different. You should have no difficulty taking care of it when we travel. I have a little surprise for you, too. Hope you will like it." He kept on walking next to her toward the car, grinning from ear to ear.

"Well, what's your surprise? Why are you being so mysterious?"

"My surprise isn't quite reality yet, but it is in a developmental stage so to speak." He got behind the wheel of the 1973 Cutlass Salon and reached into the breast pocket of his jacket, handing her the purchase agreement for the condo.

"What is this?" Laura had become almost gun shy looking at anything that resembled some sort of a legal document. He instantly recognized her trepidation holding the papers in her hand.

"I bought a condo in Fraser. I hope you don't think I'm nuts. It will be a cute little place, our own little hideaway. It will be a spot where we can get away from the world and enjoy ourselves." He wasn't facing her as he was presenting his recitation of rationales for what he ultimately would term "Hektor's Folly."

Hektor finally had the guts to look at her. He could tell immediately Laura was just as excited about the prospect of having their own little home in the mountains as he was. Tears of joy were running down her face.

"Well, tell me all about it. Where exactly is it located? What is it like? How are we going to pay for it?" He proceeded to spell out the answer to her last question first. It was foremost in his mind ever since he wrote the check for the earnest money.

"The way I see it, we can make a killing on the house in Hinterland. I estimate we could make a profit of close to fifty percent. That's a pretty good investment in a little over eighteen months. We'll take half of the profit and pay it on the condo. The rest will give us some flexibility in terms of moving here and furnishing the condo as well. Let's rent here for a while. Who knows, it might make it easier if I take a position elsewhere in a few years."

"I knew there was a deep-seated reason for my urge to clean

the house so thoroughly. Well, it will show well. Moving to a different house in Hinterland won't hurt my feelings; I was not all that happy in this place after what we've been through. Let's look for a flat somewhere closer to campus. I am planning to go back to school and finish my degree."

As luck had it, a sixteen-hundred-square-foot upper flat was available on August 1 on Twelfth Street. The owners were a young couple with a little boy. With the addition of a few coats of paint, new drapes, and light fixtures, this apartment would do nicely. They listed the house with their favorite realtor at a price somewhat higher than they thought it might bring. Hektor and Laura visited their dear friend, Gardenia, at Lake Geneva. It was such a treat to visit Laura's "adopted" aunt. Gardenia was more like an older sister than an aunt, always full of ideas, energy, and looking toward a bright future.

They couldn't believe their eyes when they got back from Lake Geneva late that Sunday night. There was a contract on the house lying on the kitchen counter. A couple bought the house without quibbling over the asking price. They realized it was almost ten o'clock. Hektor called anyway.

"Bill, is this for real? Sorry, to be calling so late, but we figured you were waiting to hear from us. We just got home from our weekend travels."

"I told you it wouldn't be difficult to sell that house in the condition in which it is. I took the liberty and canceled the open house for the realtors scheduled for tomorrow. I presume you have no problem signing the contract? I'll be by before eight thirty tomorrow morning. You kids must live right; everything is falling into place. Sleep well. I'll see you in the morning."

As he hung up the phone, a little greed crept into Hektor's mind. *Too bad we didn't try selling the house ourselves.* They would do that the next time they had property to sell in a sellers' market. Bill made a killing at both ends for the purchase and the sale of the same house.

Well, he was a nice guy and more helpful than most realtors they encountered and was deserving of his commissions.

The people who bought the house were agreeable to a July closing date, giving Hektor and Laura a chance to redecorate the flat on Twelfth Street prior to moving in the last week in July. When the last boxes were unpacked and their contents stored away, it was time to pack the car for their first driving trip to Colorado.

The Cutlass headed west at four in the morning on August 1. Gaining the extra hour, they were hoping to be in Hideaway Park between six and seven o'clock in the evening. They were through Des Moines long before rush-hour traffic and just caught the tail end of it in Omaha. Lincoln was a cinch, and then they marveled at the wide-open spaces they learned to call "miles and miles of miles and miles." They had a late lunch at the La Paloma Mexican restaurant in Ogallala, Nebraska.

Right after picking up Interstate 76, they stopped to take pictures at the "Welcome to Wonderful Colorado" sign. As they passed Julesburg, Hektor attempted to get a local radio station. He wondered what the weather was like in Denver and in the mountains. They had noticed the blue sky had given way to gray thunder boomers. Perhaps they were headed for some stormy conditions the closer they got to the distant hills.

After switching to AM reception, they heard the bad news. During the night, a powerful rainstorm had moved through the area, causing a flash flood and the deadliest natural disaster in Colorado's history. The dead and injured numbered in the hundreds; the waters of the Big Thompson River rose in the canyon by twenty to thirty feet in no time at all; warnings issued came too late for many. What an auspicious beginning this was. They would discover the devastation occurred on the eastern slope; their future hideaway was located on the western slope of the Rockies.

They arrived safely that evening in Hideaway Park. After checking in at Building 13, Hektor walked Laura over to the building site where their unit was barely framed in. Laura agreed with him, it was a beautiful spot. They went to the *Shed* for a quick bite before they stopped at the Visions Lodge to greet Nora and Larry.

Armed with a list of Nora's Denver contacts and suppliers, they undertook a major shopping spree two days later. Property Management provided them with a "must-have list" in case they eventually wanted to put their unit on the rental market. While they weren't sure if they desired to do that, the list gave them an excellent idea of all the things they might need to purchase while in Denver.

They started out early and purchased all the furniture items at one store. Next, they bought excellent mattresses directly from a local manufacturer. When the last of the small items was checked off their list later that afternoon, they fell exhausted into the car. Hektor and Laura couldn't believe they had done it all in one day. It was a marathon shopping spree, the likes of which they never experienced before and swore they would never visit upon themselves again. But they were still young and full of energy.

The next and their last day in Hideaway Park was a spectacular summer day in the Rockies. The skies were a remarkable blue without any clouds. Hektor believed they should search out these lakes to which all the brochures called attention. They drove toward Grand Lake and discovered Lake Granby and Shadow Mountain Lake. They were much larger than envisioned, although the water levels seemed to be low. Even at their least appealing, the blue of the sky reflecting in the clear water was an impressive foreground to the snow-capped mountains lying beyond.

After driving through the touristy town of Grand Lake, they made a quick stop at Rocky Mountain National Park and had dinner at the Grand Lake Lodge. They loved sitting on the open porch commanding magnificent views of the surrounding area. It was a fitting conclusion to the first of many future summertime visits to Colorado.

Once they left the "Lake District," they passed through the towns of Granby, Tabernash, and Fraser, names that eventually would just roll off their tongues. For now, they were itsy-bitsy towns connected by beautiful vistas. All were tiny western enclaves of human habitation—some of them very rustic and old-west in the truest sense. Hektor thought "ramshackle" described them far better than any other term, but he had to admit they had a certain charm. In time, they would learn to love and see these little villages from a historic perspective.

Their madcap buying spree completed, their thoughts turned toward Hinterland. In a few days, Hektor started his third academic year at the University. Laura would be taking classes toward finishing her degree. She wanted to ease into the world of academia while still holding a part-time position.

Regular telephoning kept them informed about the progress on the condominium in Hideaway Park. The week before Thanksgiving, the Denver firm delivered the furniture and placed all items according to the Birkens' detailed floor plan. Laura and Hektor drove with their packed vehicle for sixteen hours straight. They closed on the condo on Monday afternoon and spent the next twenty-four hours cleaning and decorating. By the time they left for Hinterland on Tuesday, the place was spotless. Every knickknack was unpacked and found its proper spot; all decorations and paintings were hung. When they locked the front door, they knew they would be back in a few weeks to celebrate their first Christmas break in their love nest, the Birken Hideaway.

Nora and Larry joined them for dinner one evening. Of course, she remembered Hektor's shotgun approach to purchasing the condo without Laura's input a few months earlier. After Hektor served drinks, Nora handed Hektor a small package.

"I thought this little trinket would fit you to a tee." Hektor was curious. He opened the package quickly and laughed out loud as he read the little aspen plaque.

"Be reasonable; do it my way."

1976–1991

Chapter 6

THEY were lost in their thoughts, winding their way across Berthoud Pass and taking in the pristine beauty of the snow-laden trees against the backdrop of the brilliant white peaks of the Rockies glowing in the splendor of the rising sun. Hektor glanced over at Laura, who kept busy taking in the scenes as they moved along.

"Do you think we did the right thing by buying this place?"

"Yes! I love it, and I love the mountains. I love it all, but most of all, I love the new lease this gave us on our lives. Thank you, Love, for bringing me here. I can't wait for spring break and our return, albeit for only ten days. I hope the people who rent our love nest in our absence will appreciate it as much as you and I do. Do you think we did the right thing by putting it on the rental program?"

"We'll have to wait and see. If it goes OK, it will give us some extra play money. I'm hoping to do some traveling. This will be a much-needed boost to the pocketbook. We might be able to do certain things sooner rather than later." As the car came out of the last curve, leaving National Forest territory, they noted the sign "Come Back Soon." Hektor touched Laura's arm, calling attention to the sign. They responded together.

"We will!" They continued to do so each time they passed the friendly reminder. Sadly, years later, their landmark, for whatever reason, was removed.

They jumped into the spring semester with both feet. Hektor enjoyed teaching his classes, particularly his offerings in Manual Communication and Sign Language, an area in which he became involved out of necessity after starting his teaching and clinical career at the university in the fall of 1974. Hektor remembered well how it all had begun.

⋈

Just before the end of his second semester at Hinterland, in spring 1975, a young mother had made an appointment with Hektor to discuss educational options for her little boy. He was not quite four years old and had not been responsive to any approaches provided to him. After a thorough hearing evaluation, Hektor asked mother and child to have further discussions in his comfortable office. The mother looked anguished and spoke with trepidation in her voice.

"He doesn't respond to the use of hearing aids, his drills in lip reading, etc. I took him to the School for the Deaf and knew I couldn't leave Terrance in that place. He's much too young to be that far away from me. He would be lucky to be coming home once a month. His brothers and I would miss him terribly, and he would be lost without us in his daily routine. What about using sign language? Do you use it here? Is there someone here that might work with Terrance using sign language?" Hektor had to confess.

"I'm so sorry. The program where I obtained my PhD didn't believe in sign language; 'sign' was viewed as a 'four-letter word.' But you awakened my curiosity. I'm certainly open to learning new things. I'm finishing with a large group of graduate students right now. Let me ask if any students might be interested in studying sign language during the upcoming semester break. If this should work out, we'll start Terrance in the clinic in June. I've got all the information I need from you. I'll be in touch in a few days."

The boy's mother almost hugged him; she was elated that Hektor was willing to try a new and different approach to teaching her little boy. Hektor looked pensive as he returned to his quiet office. *Why not? It will keep me busy during the break.*

When Hektor posed the question in class, several students volunteered and expressed an interest in learning fundamentals of signing during the break. Hektor opted to work with a young man; his name was Gary. Hektor got two copies of the "Joy of Signing," and he and Gary met three times a week for the purpose of practicing signing and testing each other in the language of silence.

"This is a lot of fun, Dr. B. I had no idea how involved I would become; I practice my finger spelling whenever I have a chance. Sometimes I walk around the house or on the street and just spell the words denoting anything in my visual field. Some nights, my hands are really sore, but I don't mind. I can't wait for the start of the summer semester and working with Terrance."

Hektor and Gary agreed to use one of the currently used sign systems, which allowed Gary to use English word order in the presentation of his questions or statements directed at Terrance in sign. American Sign Language uses syntax different from English and might have been too challenging for clinician and student during the initial therapy sessions.

Gary and Terrance became quite the pair to behold; their partnership was like a marriage made in heaven. Dr. B. made sure every therapy session was videotaped and subject to review with his student. About six weeks into summer school, Hektor and Gary got the shock of their lives. Gary had placed all sorts of objects all over the therapy room and asked Terrance using sign and speech simultaneously where the objects were placed. Terrance had no difficulty responding appropriately to the many questions. The next task was for Terrance to take his turn and ask Gary the same questions. Terrance spoke and signed as well.

"Where is the pen pink?" he asked, but immediately waved his hands frantically wanting to nullify his request and spoke and signed again.

"Where is the pink pen?"

Both clinician and supervisor were stunned at the child's ability to self-correct after such a short exposure to language. Here was this little boy who just a mere six weeks earlier had a vocabulary of a few words, highly visible on the lips, such as "baby, banana, boat, ball," but had no way of communicating. Terrance had discovered in a matter of weeks the magic of language usage. Hektor had tears running down his face when Gary and Terrance walked out of the therapy room. Terrance looked at him and signed.

"Why are you crying, Dr. B.?"

"Because you are so smart."

Hektor knew right then and there he would like the challenge that had presented itself so serendipitously. He loved the idea of learning the language of the deaf. Hektor and Gary kept practicing with all sorts of other books. Dr. B. had made up his mind that he would be teaching his first sign course within a year.

He fell in love with the concept of "total communication" and became known in the community as a proponent of the use of sign with profoundly deaf children who were incapable of learning language through the oral method of teaching alone. He discovered early in his career that each child needed to be treated according to specific needs; and for some children, using only amplification and lip reading was not enough to promote maximum learning capacity.

The creator of one of the more popular sign systems was a guest lecturer invited by Hektor to make a presentation to students and parents that fall. The man introduced himself and gave a short summary to the attendees. He largely signed. Terrance was seated in the front row with his mother. Hektor was behind a video camera recording the session for posterity. Terrance's eyes were glued to the man's hands and lips. After a few minutes of watching him intently, he shouted and signed.

"Use your voice." The presenter and all in attendance were shocked into disbelief. Hektor never looked back; he knew he was on the right track.

The following year, in fall of 1976, Hektor began offering his first course in manual communication. It became one of the more popular classes on campus. Eventually, he taught at least two sections each semester, which was followed by a class in advanced studies. Hektor had found his stage indeed.

He loved teaching sign and the students loved learning it with him. The highlight of each course was the finals where students presented a song and a personal story completely in sign. The joy for Hektor was that he had students from every discipline on campus taking his sign classes. In time, American Sign Language (ASL) was recognized as an acceptable substitute for the foreign language requirement. It was a battle but, sooner or later, the powers that be conceded and made Hektor's dream a reality.

But this was spring 1977. Laura, having overcome her first shock of returning to academia, was loving her learning experiences as a nontraditional student. Hektor was proud of all her successes and rewarding experiences. However, not all that happened that year was of a positive nature. Both Hektor and Laura learned that there would be sadness at times in their newly found happy lives.

Laura and Hektor's spirits were dampened when they learned Grandfather Nordstrum had suddenly passed away. He lived to be eighty-seven and was of sound mind and spirit until the day he was taken. Laura would miss his gentle ways of talking and the arrival of his weekly letters that always included poignant poetry. The kindly old gentleman sat at his trusted old typewriter composing his thoughtful epistles religiously every week, making enough copies for his daughters and Laura, the only grandchild who wrote often to her grandparents. He would truly be missed.

⋊⋉

Within days of Helena's seventieth birthday, she wrote to let Hektor know his father was hospitalized. Hektor picked up the phone in Hideaway Park and called her.

"Hello Mother. Thanks for letting me know about Dad. What seems to be wrong with him this time?"

"It's some intestinal issue, which he has battled many times. I'm sure he will be fine in a few days. I do not want you to make a special trip right now."

"Are you sure?"

"Yes. I think he'll be all right."

"On another subject then, I'm glad you liked the painting I did for your birthday."

"Yes, I liked the Colorado landscape very much and was relieved that there were no boats of any kind in your piece of art."

"Mother, how could I forget? Let me know if there is anything I can do now to help. As we discussed in Hinterland, I will not come for a funeral but would certainly come if I could assist with Dad's care."

"I can accept that. Thank you for calling."

He could read between the lines; he learned to realize when his mother wasn't willing to accept certain of his ideas.

"Give my best to Dad. Goodnight. Love you!" Helena had hung up.

Being assured by his mother his father would recover once again, it came as a shock when he learned he suddenly died after surgical intervention. When he saw Helena's handwriting on the black-rimmed envelope, he knew immediately what had happened. When he reached her by phone, he was guarded in his approach. He did not want to get into an argument with his mother.

"Why didn't anyone call us?" was his opening question. He realized immediately it was the wrong thing to say.

"What difference would it have made? I respected your wishes and didn't want to waste my money on a long-distance phone call. I knew you wouldn't make an emergency trip here to stand by me as I was burying your father. I was glad to have Albert and his family with me. Their support sustained me through the last few weeks." Hektor could read the sarcasm between the lines. He decided not to push his luck. He let his mother have the last word. Perhaps he could be of more use to her the following year.

"I am grateful that Albert and Margarethe could be there for you. We will see you next summer when we're off from school."

"OK, Hektor. Goodbye!"

Hektor knew Field Marshal Helena Birken had sprung into action. As so often in her life, she practiced the tactic of divide-and-conquer. Hektor observed it many times in the last thirty years. Sooner or later, all those who loved her, and whom she should have loved, fell victim to her scheme. If it wasn't her own siblings and their spouses or the sibling of her husband, then it was the relationship between her sons, or the relationship between Hektor and the Beerenbaums, and worst of all, the divisive attitude toward Albert and his wife and son. Hektor went to the kitchen and poured himself a double scotch; Laura knew that tranquility base was shaken.

"Guess what? Right now, we are on the top of her shit list, especially I. But don't let it bother you too much. She'll snap out of it. She'll find a more convenient victim for her tirades in no time, and we'll be relegated to inactive status. I am sorry I didn't get to see my father again. I accepted these possibilities when I chose to live in the

New World. Well, here's to you, Papa. I hope you will be happier where you are now. I always loved you; you were a real Mensch."

It was high time for Hektor to feel the touch of the silver Madonna. Laura could tell he was fighting tears. She walked over to him and hugged him fiercely. She knew he was hurting. They were glad to have each other.

〤

When the phone rang a few weeks later, Hektor couldn't believe his ears after he discovered it was his mother calling; she was so darn tight with her money. There was no greeting; she spoke in a commando voice.

"I know you have all the old audio tapes, and I demand that you search for any fragments where your father spoke a greeting or made some comments."

"OK, Mother. It's going to take me some time, but I will take care of it as soon as possible. I will send you the master copy. Is there anything else I can do?"

"No, thank you. That's all I really want—and I want it soon."

"Will do. It's going to be a big project. Take care."

"Auf wiedersehen, Hektor." She hung up before Hektor could say good-bye.

"Did I hear your mother say 'I demand …'?"

"You got that right! I'll be the dutiful son and acquiesce to her unreasonable wishes. I will spend hours editing all those damn tapes. Call it a labor of love." As soon as he finished the master tape, he sent it to his mother. He was glad to be done with that thankless job.

〤

One month later to the day, Laura's dad passed away. His death was a blessing. He and the family had dealt with his early-onset Alzheimer's disease for more than ten years. Family and friends gathered at the house on Kurtis Road, putting on a positive face by remembering the good times enjoyed when they were all younger. Dad loved memorable moments in life. Telling humorous stories involving him was a most suitable manner in which to memorialize him; he would have liked his wake.

⋈

Christmas at "Tranquility Base" in Winter Park was what they needed by the end of this year. They ushered in 1978 quietly—they thought.

"Let's go skiing today. The Broncos are playing. Few skiers will be on the slopes."

"I will need to cover my mouth. It is too windy. You think my bandana will work?"

"Sure. I'm glad Ron and Cathy are joining us. We haven't seen them in years." Everyone enjoyed the day of skiing. Laura and Cathy served the appetizers and were setting the dinner table.

"Hektor, I believe Laura isn't feeling well," Cathy observed suddenly. Hektor touched Laura's shoulder.

"What's wrong with you? Do you feel sick?" Laura just stared at him.

"Where am I? Who are you? And who are these people?" Hektor realized Laura was in serious trouble. He called the doctor in the neighboring unit. He examined Laura and spoke.

"Have you looked outside? It's a regular blizzard. Nevertheless, I suggest you get her to Presbyterian Medical Center in Denver ASAP." Ron was getting into his jacket.

"You follow me. I know exactly where it is. Let's get her into a warm jacket and get going."

They were on their way in no time flat. Hektor was glad he could follow Ron. Laura was completely out of it. She was sitting next to him—moaning. As Hektor reached the summit of Berthoud pass, Laura began to heave. The projectiles hit every orifice on the dashboard of his brand-new Olds. He really didn't care. Within seconds Laura began to speak. The act of vomiting had done the trick. It broke the spell.

"I'm sorry about your car. I feel so much better right now!" were Laura's first meaningful words.

"Never mind the dumb car. It's all plastic and can be washed. I'll stop at the little store at the bottom of the pass. I'm sure they'll let me have some wet paper towels. I'll wash your face and clean you up some. I'm glad the snow stopped. We'll be in Denver in 45 minutes."

They made it safely to the hospital; Laura was diagnosed with an acute hemiplegic migraine. The physicians confirmed her vomiting helped greatly. She was kept for 24-hour observation and dismissed the following day. Hektor breathed more easily. He was glad it was not a repeat of the stroke Laura had in 1969. He gladly undertook the cleaning and restoration of the car at their friends' home.

※

In late January, Hektor's department finally moved from an old building to their new location. After their return from a perfect spring break in Winter Park, Hektor was appointed Acting Head of the Department for the next year and a half.

The long-planned trip with their gourmet club friends became reality in May. It was a great adventure through Germany, Austria, Switzerland, Italy, and France; the grand finale was a visit in Köndringen and a reunion with Aunt Klara.

Albert and Margarethe joined the Amis (Americans) at the Lion Inn. Aunt Klara had sold the Lion several years earlier to a younger couple. What used to be Uncle Rudi's workshop became Aunt Klara's modern apartment. She could live there for the rest of her days. The Shell station was gone, and the inn was modernized and expanded. Only the outside retained its five-hundred-year-old appearance. Aunt Klara took charge in that now much-beloved sing-songy voice.

"I'm so happy to see both of you boys—and your wives to boot. Forgive me, I shouldn't call you boys. You are both grown men. How I loved having you when you were boys indeed." She smiled at Hektor.

"Hand your camera to one of your Ami friends. Have them take a photo of us in front of the Lion. I'll treasure it." Aunt Klara looked and sounded the same; only her thick hair had turned snow white. It was a reunion none ever forgot; it was a journey all talked about from then on.

⋊

Eventually, Albert, Margarethe, Laura, and Hektor arrived in Essen. Mother Birken was anxiously awaiting them. Alone at last with Hektor and Laura, Helena fired her first shot.

"It's high time you finally made an appearance here. Personally, I thought you would visit me right away. Was it necessary to do all this gallivanting through the Alpine countries with your friends before seeing me? I believe your first responsibilities were here."

"C'est la vie," thought Hektor. The next day, Mother Birken pressed for a visit to the cemetery; in her opinion, it was a long-overdue event. Margarethe joined them. Hektor stood with his wife, mother, and sister-in-law in front of the immaculately manicured cemetery plot of his father. The wind had blown a few dried leaves off one of the rhododendron bushes, spoiling the gravesite in Helena's mind.

"Margarethe, fetch the rake from behind the grave marker. Pick up this leaf, pick up that leaf, and be sure to rake the unsightly footprints you are leaving behind in the process." The tone of voice in which his sister-in-law was commanded to execute totally unnecessary actions blew Hektor's mind. Being used to Helena's wrath, Margarethe simply complied. Helena stared at her son.

"Aren't you going to say anything to your father? The least you could do is say some kind of prayer for the dead." Helena's demands were almost insulting to Hektor. He already had said a quiet prayer for his father, believing it inappropriate to make a public spectacle of himself.

It galled him how his mother was carrying on about his father, the man with whom she had battled for forty-seven years. All of a sudden, she was acting as if their relationship was the love feast of the century. All Hektor could recall were the ugly scenes, the constant fighting over nonexistent moneys, the fault-finding with his dad, and the ever-present disharmony that drove Hektor off to seek his own happiness in another world. He had crossed an ocean to get away from them and their daily tribulations.

"What do you expect me to do? I won't genuflect. You act as if you and Dad always enjoyed a loving relationship. Maybe it's something you experienced during your last years. I'm sorry, but it isn't anything I ever observed myself. My memories are different from those you seem to have. I loved my father very much; I have to mourn his passing in my private way. I can't conduct myself in ways just to please your fancy. Furthermore, I said my prayer quietly as soon as we arrived here."

Helena took it all in. She marched off toward the parked car. All of them knew that the first visit to the cemetery was concluded. That night, Hektor turned to his mother.

"I would like to use your typewriter; I have this need to put some of my thoughts on paper. You mind? I'll go to our bedroom and close the door. I'm sure the sound from the typewriter won't disturb you."

"Go right ahead. I keep the typewriter in the room where you and Laura are staying. You'll see it; it sits on the bottom shelf of my bookcase. It should work well. I recently had it serviced and a new ribbon installed. You go right ahead; Laura and I will have a glass of wine."

Hektor did as he was told and found the typewriter right away. He closed the door and sat down to write. He rolled the first sheet of paper into the machine and began to type.

"I Remember Papa—A Letter to My Dead Father"

Dear Father, or should I say Papa? That's what I called you most of the time. How does one write a letter to one's dead father? I feel almost like Hamlet, writing a soliloquy. When I add up the years that I actually lived with you, they number less than ten. It was so little time to spend with you. Now that I page through my memories, I feel a close kinship. I can see much of you in myself. The hours and days spent together made a more profound impression on me than I realized. Where does one begin?

You were much too young to die. Within weeks of Mother's seventieth birthday, I received the envelope with the black rim. I recognized her handwriting immediately; I knew what the content would be. Pronouncements of death never came in plain envelopes.

At age forty-three, one would think I knew you well. You were always a big man. From my point of view, you were huge. Although temperamental and often volatile, you were basically a gentle man. You were a Mensch, as my Jewish friends would say. I often wondered how someone as gentle as you could function as a butcher. I remember how you loved the arts, especially music. On many occasions, I thought you were professionally misplaced. But then, these choices were usually made by one's parents. I can speak from personal experience.

Some of my earliest recollections of you, dear father,

take me back to the magic days of radio. I can still hear you compete with Beniamino Gigli or Richard Tauber in some German rendition of arias from *La Bohème* or *La Traviata*, attempting to drown out the incessant noise of the machines in the *Wurstküche* [sausage kitchen].

I was a mere child of five when you were taken away from us and sent to the front in Poland. It was difficult to imagine how a gentle giant of a man could kill any other human being. What a dreadful mission. While your trade might have primed you for killing enemies, it actually sheltered you from doing so. You knew how to deal in large quantities of foods and liked to cook. Serving as a cook in the army saved you from fighting and killing. Deep down, you must have been happy.

When you came home for that short furlough in 1941, you didn't brag about the number of enemies you had killed. Instead you surprised us with the biggest fowl we had ever seen. Albert and I couldn't get over the size of the dead bird you had wrapped in your dirty clothes, transporting it all the way from Poland. Much later in America, the creature, known there as "turkey," was reintroduced to me as the annual traditional food for Thanksgiving. Of course, who knew in 1941 that someday an ocean would separate our lives?

By 1942, you found yourself lying flat on your back at the elegant "Badischer Hof" in Baden-Baden. The nuns of the Cistercian order took such good care of you. It was through your contact with Uncle Rudi that we wound up being sheltered in little Köndringen by Aunt Klara. How we loved being so close to you and our visits to see you.

When Mother insisted on taking us back to the terrors of war, you were opposed to the idea; but she was always the stronger and more willful of the two of you. I'm sorry she never let you be the man you could have been. It was a classic example of Mother being the pragmatist and you not being able to deal with reality.

We suffered with you in Mother's bomb shelter on the night of September 23, 1944. You tried shielding us from the horrors of life-threatening bombs. Eventually you were the one who insisted that all of us seek safety in a more substantial underground bunker, as difficult as the challenge was for you to hobble that distance.

Time has blurred many of the happenings of those final months during World War II. However, I vividly remember the night of New Year's Eve 1944. There were no bomb attacks during the holidays. Indeed, the enemies kept their word, and all was quiet on the home front. You and I went to hear the words of wisdom by our "great leader." It was as cold a night as I can ever remember; it was bitterly cold. The stars were so bright, I thought I could touch them. I remember my question: "Dad, why are the stars so bright tonight?" as we were making our way to the shelter. You said it was because of the total blackout that the stars could shine all the brighter. That was telling.

Walking side by side with you, all I could hear was the thump, thump, thump of your crutches and boots touching the frozen ground. The experience is so indelibly engraved on my mind that, no matter how often I walk on other bitterly cold nights under starry skies with the crunch of frozen snow beneath my feet, I'm always taken back to that scene all so long ago.

Oh, I remember the tantrums you would have when you were ill and the one and only time you struck me when you were utterly disgusted with my unsuitable behavior. Mother was a great one for using physical punishment to keep us growing boys in check. You used less physical than vocal persuasion. Sometimes, your choleric tirades were harder to take than Mother's swift vengeance.

My relationship to the Beerenbaums caused many ugly scenes with Mother; you were actually more hurt than jealous. Reportedly, you grew up in a loving environment. Unlike you, Mother was reared in a milieu where everything revolved around success in business and money. The Krämers were driven by the need for amassing wealth, and most of its members became quite good at it. Money begot money by earning or marrying it; in their eyes, anyone who did not fit the mold was to be pitied. Unfortunately for Mother, you were not a businessman.

I was glad that you and Mom committed to the adventure of a lifetime and visited us in America. Mother was impressed with my doctor title; you loved what I was doing with little deaf children. You were happy for me that I had found my niche in life at last, be it ever so far away from you.

I vividly recall my last conversation with you, still being overpowered by the fragrance of the giant lilac bouquet that stood between us that afternoon in Hinterland. I wanted to thank you for the person you allowed me to become. Again and again I wanted to get up and tell you how much I loved you—but I didn't. I let the opportunity pass. Tears are in my eyes as I recall that afternoon. That invisible wall I created in past years let us part forever without my having said the words "I love you, Father."

In retrospect, I'm glad I was spared the agony of seeing you dead. Did I deprive myself of dealing with your death? Perhaps. I shall never know. As I think of you at this moment, the image I see before my eyes is as I remember you best. There must have been more negative experiences between us than I seem to recall. Strangely enough, they have vanished from my repertoire of collected memories. Perhaps, subconsciously, I choose to see you only in the most flattering light. Just let me hear some familiar strains from a Puccini or Verdi opera, then the lifeline is unbroken—and I remember you, Papa. Farewell, dear father and friend. May you be at peace at last. Always remember I loved you.

⋈

Hektor took the last page he had typed out of the clunky old typewriter and opened the door. It was past two o'clock in the morning. His mother had gone to bed hours ago; Laura was curled up and sound asleep on the living room sofa. He kissed her and gently wakened her.

"Come to bed. I'm finally done. I simply had this need to put down my thoughts and feelings on paper."

"Your mother was very upset with you for leaving us to fend for ourselves and typing whatever for hours on end. She was hoping you didn't expect her to read your diatribe. That was the last thing on her mind. Actually, she was very much hurt when she bid me goodnight."

"Well, I didn't write it for her benefit or blessing; I wrote it for myself, having this need to communicate with the dead man and wishing to recall and remember the fragments of my life with the man who was my father. You can read the pages sometime, perhaps on the plane when we are heading home."

⋈

Early the next morning, Helena and Hektor had another confrontation. He had gone to the WC to shave off his beard, a bone of contention with his mother. He had failed to turn the key on the lavatory door. Helena walked in on Hektor and saw him standing bare chested in front of the mirror. Apparently, she noticed immediately that Hektor wasn't wearing Greta's silver Madonna.

"I'm glad you are no longer wearing that damn Catholic thing around your neck. It's high time you saw the light. And get rid of that ugly old beard. Why do you insist on irritating me every chance you get?"

"As far as the beard is concerned, I'm shaving it off to please myself; it's too darn hot here this summer. Greta's silver Madonna is still with me; she just isn't hanging from my neck any longer."

Shaking her head in disgust, she walked out and slammed the door. Hektor and Laura were glad to escape from the gloom and doom of his mother's home to visit Albert and his family, his aunts, the Beerenbaums, and the Gunders. At the breakfast table, she handed Hektor the coup de grace.

"My friend tells me you made mistakes in creating the recording of your father's utterances. The tape is useless. You will have to do it again when you return to the States. I insist on having these recordings. I know you have all those tapes we made. Those utterances by your father will comfort me and keep me closer to him in my loneliness."

"Bullshit! Where is the tape now? I could play it and see for myself. Perhaps you pushed the wrong buttons when you tried to listen to it."

"My friend has it at his house. He is gone and won't be back until after your departure. If you came here first instead of traveling with your American friends, you might have met my gentleman caller. You simply have to take my word for it. Do the job again, and this time, do it correctly. It won't hurt you to dedicate a few more hours of your precious time to your departed father and me."

"Bullshit! Bullshit! Go screw yourself, lady!"

He was glad his mother didn't understand his outburst. Laura knew he was angry when she heard his language. She could sense the tension. Eventually, he tried to control himself. When he shook his fist behind Helena as she stormed out of the room, Laura could tell by the color of his knuckles how seriously he detested the scene with his mother. Laura knew he had no intention of wasting his time. He had tested the tape before sending it to Helena.

They visited Albert and his family in the afternoon. Helena took out her feelings of displeasure on all who were present. Hektor slammed his fist on the marble coffee table, glaring at his mother.

"Don't you dare treat your grandson and his date in this despicable manner! The burr on your saddle for which I'm supposedly responsible doesn't excuse your behavior. Sometimes I don't believe what I'm seeing!"

Helena didn't respond. She didn't like being put in her place in front of a total stranger. The tone for the evening and the remaining days was set. Mother Birken sank once again into the depths of negativism consistent with her dual personality. It was sheer hell for all of them.

The morning of their departure, Hektor put two hundred-mark bills under a vase sitting on the buffet in the living room. The top of the buffet still bore the inscription *Vive La France* made by a Frenchman's bayonet during the waning days of World War II. Hektor wished it said, *Vive la paix* [Long live peace]. Saying their goodbyes, Hektor turned to his mother.

"Please use the money I left on the buffet to buy flowers or plantings for dad's grave as needed."

"Where, where . . . is the money? Oh, I see it." She grabbed the bills. She almost knocked over the large vase, a gift from her sister Elsa. She threw the bills into Hektor's face.

"I don't want your money and certainly not to buy flowers for your father's grave. I am done with you; you are no son of mine." Laura began to cry. Once again, she faced another of Helena's tirades as she and Hektor departed from Germany. It was just too much for her. She was not used to such conduct in her family or in her relationship with Hektor. He turned to Margarethe, giving her the money.

"Perhaps you will take care of this for me. I would appreciate you buying some flowers for Dad as you see fit." Hektor's mother was reaching for the bills in Margarethe's hands; she had every intention of ripping the bills into shreds but didn't succeed.

"If you dare put anything on his grave bought with that money, I will tear it out with my bare hands." Her face was distorted and her teeth flashing, not unlike those of a mad dog. All of them retreated as fast as possible. This behavior from his mother was the final straw.

⋊⋉

They sat silently in Albert's Mercedes as it swiftly carried them to the airport in Frankfurt. The girls made their teary goodbyes. Hektor and Albert agreed; it was, once again, one hell of a visit.

"We'll call you when we get home. I won't write to Mother. She will have to apologize to Laura and me before she will ever hear from us again." They hugged before they walked down the gangplank.

⋊⋉

Returning from a professional meeting in San Francisco in late November, Hektor sorted his way through the bulk of the accumulated mail. There was a letter from Helena. He tore it open.

"My *dear* son, *dear* Laura! I want to sincerely apologize for my unseemly behavior when you visited me last summer. Since then, I have discovered that my equipment rather than your tape was at fault. I'm hoping you didn't take the time to redo the recordings."

Of course, she hadn't needed to worry about that! Not in his wildest dreams had Hektor considered doing that yeoman's job a second time. He couldn't help gloating over his mother's apology.

"You need to write to her right away," was Laura's opinion.

"Not so quick. I am going to let her stew a little. I have not forgotten the way we were treated just before our departure a few months ago." Hektor collected his thoughts to write the annual Christmas letter.

"Please be forgiving and write to your mother. Don't be as thick-headed as she is," pleaded Laura. Eventually he heeded her advice.

Mother Birken's Christmas package arrived in time for the holidays, bearing gifts of marzipan, fancy chocolates, and German baked specialties. They were at peace at last. They couldn't wait to usher in 1979 at their beloved hideaway.

Chapter 7

SUMMER vacation didn't come around soon enough. Being promoted to Associate Professor gave Hektor and Laura good reason for celebrating their arrival at Tranquility Base.

"During this semester break, we must make a journey east. We need to visit the children. Your grandson, Peter Jans, will be almost one year old. Obviously, you are not quite ready to be called 'grandpa.' However, that is what you are. Frank and Karen are your responsibility. I want you to take a more personal interest in your family. In spring 1981, we need to spend time with those kids while you are on sabbatical at the Rochester Institute of Technology. Perhaps we could get to know them better now that they are adults."

"I planned to visit RIT, if for no other reason than to check out the housing situation. We could see your Mom traveling through Detroit. It might be fun to touch base with our friends in upstate New York. I concur; we do need to see the kids. We saw Frank last before he went into the Navy in 1974. Gosh, time has flown."

Upon their arrival in New York, Hektor and Laura were greeted by the entire Unkovsky clan assembled at Georgia's house. Hektor had a difficult time dealing with the thickness of schmaltz being spread around by his former spouse. It used to just grate on him when she would write, "My *very dear* Laura, my *very dear* Hektor." He never thought their relationship had ever been "very dear" after they said "I do."

It was truly amazing to him how Georgia could be so hypocritical after all they experienced in their stormy four-year relationship. Yet, when he thought about it seriously, she never did live in the real world. Life was one constant fantasy after another for her, always conducting herself as if she had been raised in the gutter. Having failed at two marriages at this point in time, she was chatting about searching for number three. So far, she had four children by three different men. Hektor couldn't wait to get away from her. They drove to the Swansong home. Estelle greeted them excitedly.

"How wonderful to see you both again! Come in. I want to hear all about your visit with the clan." Estelle wasn't a gossip, but she loved hearing about the continuing soap opera of "Hektor and Georgia." She was right. It was like a soap opera. Some of the happenings were indeed stranger than fiction. Hektor and the Swansongs had reason to celebrate; it had been 25 years since they first met.

On their way back to Detroit, they spent the afternoon in Rochester. The National Technical Institute for the Deaf (NTID) was a fascinating site. Hektor knew he would love spending his sabbatical there. They were shown faculty housing units that would suffice during their five-month stay less than two years hence.

"I'll make it homey. I'll love playing house. It will be a great opportunity for me to relax a little. Those apartments aren't really that bad. You'll see." Laura was the eternal optimist.

At the end of the fall term, they were both looking forward to being with Hektor's family in Germany. He never was certain about what to expect as far as his mother was concerned but was always hoping for the best. Having flown into Frankfurt, they were met by Albert and Margarethe.

"Mother is looking forward to your visit. She is in one of the best moods we've experienced with her in a long time. She likes going to the office and enjoys the companionship of an elderly gentleman. We don't know much about him; but as we all know, mother is happiest when she has someone to worry and fuss about. He seems to be good for her disposition. Perhaps she has found a willing new victim in the gentleman caller."

Albert was right; their mother was in excellent spirits. For once, they had peaceful and joyous gatherings while in the old country. Perhaps it was a good omen that she wasn't totally focused on her immediate family. Albert and Hektor were shocked by the generous gift of money she handed them after dinner on Christmas Eve.

"Mom, what's this all about? You are being far too lavish with your Christmas presents for us."

"I want you to have some extra spending money on your trip to Austria. It always costs more money going on such a vacation. My sincere wish is that all four of you have a marvelous time being together." *Were they listening to their mother?* They had no idea what epiphany she experienced. Helena was definitely in one of her upward spirals.

They left three days before New Year's Eve for their cross-country skiing vacation in the Ramsau area of Austria. After an overnight stay at a charming pension, they arrived at their destination and couldn't believe their eyes. There wasn't a snowflake on the ground or in sight. The only place where there was snow and ice was on the slopes of the mighty *Dachstein* with an elevation of not quite ten thousand feet. Disappointment was written on all faces.

"What are we going to do now? This is not exactly what the

brochures promised us. I guess we'll walk and eat and drink a lot," was Albert's assessment of the sad situation. Hektor's approach was different.

"I suggest all of us do some serious praying." His brother glared back at him, underscoring his disbelief in prayer by placing his hands on his hips as if such a stance would defy the power of the Almighty.

"You must be joking! Praying? Who believes in such hogwash? And for snow?" As they were leaving for their New Year's celebration dinner, they were greeted by giant snowflakes fluttering through the air.

Waking up in the morning, they discovered the answer to prayers. There were more than two feet of perfect snow on the ground, and the village "track master" had already laid perfectly formed tracks for cross-country skiing throughout the entire valley. Next to the tracks was a walking lane as well as a path for horse-drawn sleighs. It was perfection in winter wonderland. They loved having their pictures taken beside the frequently encountered signs, reminding them that cross-country skiers lived longer.

The vacation was everything the Birken sons and their wives had dreamed about—and more.

Hektor and Laura fell in love with the cozy little taverns and tiny inns all along the many trails they were exploring. One of their favorite places was the *Halseralm Inn*, a rustic old barn that offered wonderful Austrian specialties and drinks on their menu. The only thing one had to watch out for was not to have too many of their alcoholic surprises. Getting off the *Alm* and back into the flats of the valley could be a challenge if one was the slightest bit tipsy. It was a vacation all liked so well, they made a point of planning to return a few years later.

Their transatlantic flight was uneventful. They faced a severe midwestern winter. Laura returned to her studies. She chose heavy loads during the last year of undergraduate work and was determined to finish her student teaching by early February 1981.

"I want to join you in Rochester ASAP."

⋈

By now Hektor and Laura were used to the surprises Helena sprang on them. Hektor listened carefully to her rapid announcements on the phone.

"I have purchased plane tickets. I will arrive in Minneapolis on September 1 at five o'clock in the afternoon. I am planning to be with you for the month."

"Mother, what is the reason for your impromptu visit? Don't you think you should have consulted with us before you booked a flight? We love having you, but a little more consideration would have been nice. Just imagine, we might have booked a trip ourselves and not even be home."

"Son, I still have a good mind. You have no other place to be for the month of September. You will barely have started your fall semester when I arrive. Last I knew, you still had a full-time position at the university."

"You got me there, Mom."

"I am very lonesome, and there is nothing keeping me here. It's fall and my balcony doesn't need any attention. A neighbor loves taking care of my birds and will look after my indoor plants. How often have you told me I was always welcome?"

"That's true, Mutti, but a hint might have been nice. Well, we look forward to your arrival and will meet you at the airport in Minneapolis." She was always very specific. Hektor was surprised she didn't cite her return flight. It was a bombshell they hadn't banked on. They were amazed she would undertake the trip by herself.

"What may I bring with me?"

"Whatever you do, don't bring any meat products or fruits and vegetables. And no cuttings from your Christmas cactus! That piece you stuck into the bottom of the bag with the other presents when we saw you last almost got us into big trouble. Having those things with you can get you in serious difficulties with the authorities—and us, too, for that matter."

"Well, I'll stop talking. See you on the first of September. Bye!" And she was gone.

⋊

She arrived on time, and they made an overnight stop so that Helena could meet Elaine, Charles, and their children, who were still living in Minneapolis. She had a jolly old time with Laura's family. Of course, there were offerings of chocolate and marzipan. She couldn't wait to get to Hinterland and unpack her suitcases. Hektor wasn't sure why she traveled with two large pieces of luggage. As she unpacked in Hinterland, she called for Hektor and Laura to look at one of the presents she brought them. It looked like a giant tube wrapped in one of her flannel nightgowns.

"Open it. The wrapping I will need." Unrolling the mysterious package, a giant smoked sausage emerged. It was double sealed in plastic, allowing no odors to betray the content.

"That's one, and here is another. These ought to last you for a while!"

"How could you do that, Mother? You have no idea the trouble you could've been in! Remember what I told you about entering the U.S. with contraband?"

"Oh fiddlesticks! Trouble! Contraband! I didn't smuggle weapons into the country. Just enjoy some decent German sausage. No harm done. You are not selling it or giving it to other people. Sometimes you have to take risks in life."

It sounded like the old Helena Birken of days long gone. That's how Hektor always remembered his "Mother Courage" as she fought her personal battles during World War II. In a way, it was wonderful to see her so spirited.

"I suppose you are right. We'll refrain from telling anyone about your escapades. Thanks for the tasty treats; our friends and we will enjoy them for months to come." Helena was proud as punch. She had shown them. When they retired that first evening, Helena made them laugh.

"Schlooooop you goooot!"—her one and only attempt at speaking English. She was convinced she had told them in English to sleep well. Hektor and Laura went along with it and never corrected her. As much as she liked to flaunt her knowledge of French, the English language didn't do it for her.

Their friends were treated to *Zwiebelkuchen* [onion pie], *Sauerbraten*, *Rouladen*, and *Spätzle*, and the latest recipe of *Käsekuchen* [cheesecake].

"I brought you this wonderful new cheesecake recipe, Laura. We'll shop for the ingredients and bake one for the elegant party at the house of your friends, the Chinese doctor and his family." Helena, Hektor, and Laura went to the neighborhood grocery store to do some major shopping. She was intrigued by all the neatly packaged items in the store.

"This cheese will work perfectly. It looks like our *Quark* in Germany," Helena said as she pointed at cartons of cottage cheese.

"Are you sure you won't need ricotta instead?" inquired Laura.

"No, this will work just fine. We also need a lot of eggs. The other thing I want to buy is the meat for our Sauerbraten." Approaching the meat department, her eagle eyes spotted a huge hunk of meat.

"This piece of beef contains the hip from which I would like to get a good cut. I don't want this end or that. What I need is the piece right out of the middle."

Hektor overheard her gibberish about the meat and intervened.

"Mother, they will only sell you the whole piece. They'll never cut out the exact piece you are describing to Laura."

"What kind of butchers do you have in America? Don't they

know how to use a knife and cut the proper cuts of meat one needs for fixing certain dishes? Just push that button and summon the young butcher. Explain to him what I need. They can repackage the rest. No one will ever know the difference." Hektor did as he was told and explained to the young man behind the counter what his mother wanted. With a sheepish expression on his face, Hektor informed the meat cutter that his mother had grown up in a butcher's family in Germany.

"I don't care what they do in Germany. Here, it's done differently. Tell her if she wants that particular piece, she'll have to buy the whole hunk. Take it or leave it." With that he attempted to walk away.

"Junger Mann, kommen Sie zurück" [Young man, come back here], she shouted in German as Hektor quickly tried to convey to her the gist of his conversation with the butcher.

The young butcher was actually kind of cute, thought Laura, as he turned around and faced Helena. She didn't even give him a chance to say another word. Helena spoke and mimed with her whole body and hands what she wanted from him. He thought he was looking at Rumpelstiltskin. The butcher stood there, not believing what he saw. He picked up the hunk of meat, carrying it back to his butcher block. Hektor understood him mumbling.

"Lady, you are one piece of work. I'll go along with your fuckin' idea, but it will cost you dearly."

"What did he say to me just then?" Helena wanted to know. Hektor thought a lie would serve him best.

"He said he was happy to oblige as long as you had pleaded your case so convincingly." Walking back into the store, the young man carried three pieces. One of them was exactly what Helena had demanded. He handed it to her grinning shamefacedly.

"I hope you are happy now, but it's really going to cost you!" She didn't understand a word he was saying but she was happy! She turned triumphantly toward Hektor and Laura.

"You see, I achieved exactly what I had in mind, and I don't even have to speak English to do it." She didn't care how much it cost and marched off with the shopping cart, leaving Hektor, Laura, and the young butcher shrugging their shoulders. It was once again perfect Helena Birken.

)(

Helena and Laura whipped up the cheesecake, getting it promptly into the oven. As soon as the cheesecake started to bake, Laura cleaned the kitchen counter in preparation for the turning of the cheesecake once it emerged from the oven. Helena couldn't wait to spring into action.

"Let's turn it over right away, allowing the cake to cool in that position." They did. Seconds later, Helena howled as she noticed the cake was apparently juicier than she had experienced during her dry runs in Germany.

"Laura, Laura, der Kuchen ist kaput; komm hier und guck Dir das an!" [Laura, Laura; the cake is kaput. Come and look at it!] Laura took a spatula and literally shoveled the drippy mass back into the form, dark skin and all. She patted it and stuck it back into the oven.

"No harm done. We'll just let it bake for another twenty or thirty minutes. It will be fine. After we cool it sufficiently, I'll dust it with some powdered sugar."

"We can't take that cake to those friends of yours. And if you do, please don't tell them I had anything to do with it." When the dessert was presented, Helena assumed no ownership in the creation of the "culinary masterpiece."

"Laura, how did you get this marvelous marbleized effect in the cheesecake? I want the recipe to take back with me to Hong Kong," intoned the mother of Laura's friend. Laura smiled like a Cheshire cat promising her to mail it. Helena couldn't believe these people, but she had to admit Laura's quick reinvention worked wonders. The visit went by all too fast. Helena enjoyed their home and meeting so many of their close friends.

"If I were thirty years younger and spoke the language, I could learn to live here. I really enjoyed my visit with you. The one thing that sometimes crossed my mind was what would happen if I were to become ill and even die here? What would you do?"

"Oh, Mom, that wouldn't be such a big problem. We would just have you cremated and mail your ashes to Germany in a cigar box. That wouldn't cost too much money, would it now?" She almost went into shock.

"You wouldn't do that to me, would you? You know how I feel about being buried next to your father. Cremation is out of the question. I will have to look into some special insurance if I visit you again in the future. You can really scare me."

Hektor heartily laughed, letting her know he was only trying to get a rise out of her. However, in her first letter after her return, she let him know she looked into the matter as soon as she safely arrived back in Germany.

"I called my insurance agent and he told me he would be more than happy to amend my policy with a rider that would cover such expenses were I to die while traveling. So, don't worry about keeping empty cigar boxes handy."

※

At Thanksgiving, Millie Prior was surrounded by her entire family. She was seriously considering the sale of the house on Kurtis Road. After living there for more than thirty-eight years, she would move to her condo in Florida to get away from the long and cold winters of the Midwest.

As Laura's mom played the grand piano, everyone joined in the rendition of "We Gather Together." It proved to be the last family event at the old homestead in Grosse Pointe Farms; this was the spot all three Prior girls would always consider their home. Their mother's new condo in Florida was just a nice place to visit. Time indeed had moved on.

Chapter 8

HEKTOR arrived at NTID in Rochester, NY, in early January, 1981. Their car was packed to the limit. He was actually stopped and searched when he crossed the border into Canada. The highlight of the long journey was seeing Niagara Falls once again in the depth of winter. It was indeed a spectacular sight. Laura flew in three weeks later after she finished with her student teaching. Hektor was truly enjoying his studies in American Sign Language. He was involved in several research projects and liked the colleagues with whom he was working.

On weekends, they visited friends and family all over the state and on Long Island. They planned an extensive camping trip after their stint at NTID. Their travels would take them through the New England states and all of the Maritime Provinces.

In April they received an audiotape from Albert and Margarethe. Helena was once again in one of her downward spirals and threatening to commit the ultimate deed. Hektor picked up the phone and called her.

"Mother, we heard from Albert and Margarethe. Would you mind telling me why you are talking this kind of nonsense again? You are in good health and have so much to live for. I just don't understand you. Have you discussed some of your feelings with your doctor?"

"Yes, I have. Much good that does. He has no clue how lonesome I am. Your father has been gone for four years. I'm tired of talking to my birds. My closest friends have died or are living in other parts of the country. Some don't want to have anything to do with me any longer. My gentleman caller got tired of my nagging. Since Alphons married, I only hear from him once in a while. Frankly, I'm tired of living."

"Well, what about Albert and his family? You have a wonderful grandson. I know he isn't very close to you, but that is partially your doing. Don't you think it is time for you to make up for all those lost years and try to get to know him?

"I have another idea, too. Right now, we are living just hours from the children. And Frank and Jolene have little Peter Jans. Why don't you plan to visit us while we are here in Rochester? You could meet your American grandchildren and even meet your first great-grandchild. Don't those sound like good reasons to live? What do you think?"

"Well, I don't know if I want to take another long flight. It is so far away."

"It wasn't that far last year when you surprised us. You had a marvelous time with us and our friends. You are in such great shape. I'm sure your grandchildren would love to meet you."

"Boy, you sure know how to twist my arm. OK, you talked me into this foolishness. Whatever you do, I don't want you to tell your brother about my visit to see you and the children. If you do, I will cancel the trip. I will look into getting a plane ticket to New York City. I'll write to you as soon as I know the details. I presume you and Laura will fetch me at the airport?"

"Of course, we'll pick you up. Thank you, Mother. That sounds a lot more reasonable. We'll talk about the details after we hear from you. Love you!"

Hektor was on the phone for close to an hour trying to talk Helena out of the senseless act. It probably was the most expensive telephone call he ever made. But they thought it was worth the effort. Helena's letter arrived a few days later. She was landing at JFK in New York on May 1. Her return ticket was open-ended. She could stay as long as three months.

"If you breathe a word to your brother, I will tear up these tickets."

As promised, they picked her up at the airport. On their way back to Rochester, they stopped to see the children. Peter Jans was hospitalized; he had fallen from a second-story window at his parents' home. Hektor, Laura, Helena, and Frank went to visit the little boy in the hospital. He seemed to be OK.

"How did he fall out of a second-story window? Don't they watch their little boy?" Great-grandmother wanted to know. None of the visitors were given a clue how the fall had occurred.   Frank finally confessed. Peter Jans had climbed on the window sill and pushed out the screen. They discovered his fall when they heard him screaming in much pain lying on the sidewalk in front of their house. Helena kept shaking her head after Hektor had given her the translation.

"My God, they might have lost him. I don't understand such callousness." She would have died had she known that both parents were found higher than a kite on drugs when the neighbors summoned an ambulance. Helena pointed at one of the orderlies; Laura had left the room to confer with one of the nurses in charge.

"Hektor, ask that young man to take a photo of the four of us. I would like to have it as a memento of my visit." The four-generation photo was taken by the young man. Helena treasured it for the rest of her days.

They spent a couple of days in the Birchtown area; Helena had the opportunity to meet some of Hektor's longest-standing friends in the States. Lots of stories were told; Hektor was kept busy translating. Mother Birken wished she could speak the language. It was a most enjoyable experience for her. When they arrived at NTID, Helena wondered why a tent was set up in the living room.

"I wanted you to see and be prepared for how we will be traveling with you when I get done here. Won't it be fun for the three of us to be sleeping in our igloo tent? We knew you would really love it. That flap is just about the right height for you to get comfortably inside. You want to try it?" Hektor could tell by his mother's facial expression that she thought he had lost it.

"You are joking, aren't you? You can't be serious about schlepping your seventy-four-year-old mother in a tent all over the country?"

"I am, Mom. You'll love it being so close to Mother Nature. Tenting is a lot more fun than some fancy rig parked on a concrete pad." Hektor climbed into the tent and invited his mother to join him. She finally did.

"Come sit down on this comfortable pad and see how you like it." When she went along with his scheme, Laura quickly snapped a few photos, preserving the precious moment for posterity. Hektor at last owned up to the fact he was pulling her leg. Helena breathed a sigh of relief. Laura had Mother situated in her bedroom shortly after supper. It was then that they made a quick call to Albert and Margarethe.

"Surprise! Mother is with us in New York. She swore she would cancel the trip if we told you before. She is sound asleep and snoring. We won't tell her we called. We will send postcards and keep you in the loop. Enjoy the respite." They could hear Albert and Margarethe breathing sighs of relief. Hektor started to take down the tent.

"Obviously, we'll need to alter our travel plans. I don't believe I convinced Mother to sleep with us in the North Face tent. It and all the other camping equipment we'll ship back with UPS."

Laura canceled camping reservations and booked B&Bs and hotels where necessary. Helena and her German cooking made a hit with all of Hektor's friends and colleagues at NTID. She loved it when they invited deaf students to dine with them.

The weeks at NTID were for Hektor the culmination of a great experience in his professional life; his sabbatical turned into one of the most productive periods in his career and had long-lasting effects. He knew he would be dedicated to better teaching and clinical intervention to enhance the lives of hearing-impaired and profoundly deaf children and adults. The morning they left NTID, the three of them were a sight to behold. Laura was squeezed between boxes in the backseat. Helena was in the passenger seat. She had pulled a woolen ski cap way down over her ears.

"Mother, you look like Ivan the Terrible. Why are you making that awful face?"

"Because I have no idea what's coming at me!"

"Oh Mother, you will see some of the most historic sites on the continent. Why don't you just sit back and enjoy it all!" Hektor wasn't sure his mother was capable of doing that.

Helena was impressed by the homes of the rich and famous in Newport; "The Breakers," the former home of the Vanderbilts, was among her favorites. Boston was an absolute delight. She didn't get along too well with the black flies in New Hampshire; they really gave Laura and Helena's scalps a workout. In Maine, a giant boiled lobster staring back at Helena from the dinner plate did not become her friend. She elected to try another American specialty—a hamburger.

In Montreal, Hektor and his mother came to blows. She couldn't make up her mind where she wanted her precious jewelry kept. First, the box was stored way back in the trunk. Then it had to be dug out and taken to the hotel room. Going out for dinner, it was no longer safe in the room.

"Put it back in the rear of the trunk."

"What if someone has been watching all of these maneuvers and breaks into the car? I don't know why you had to bring all that stuff with you anyway. Why the hell didn't you leave it all in your safe at home? Who are you trying to impress? Certainly not us. We are familiar with most of these pieces and their 'interesting' histories."

After Ottawa, Detroit was the last stop before they headed home to Iowa. Dinner was an absolute delight. Hektor and Laura were pleased to see their mothers together after all these years. They got along famously, neither one speaking the other's language.

Helena had a great time in Iowa—most of the time. She felt comfortable with Hektor and Laura's friends since she had met many during her previous visits. Their friends Dot and Bill invited the Birkens for dinner at a Swiss/German restaurant at a neighboring town. Helena sampled the Sauerbraten and Spaetzle with all the classic trimmings. The owner and chef made the fatal mistake of inquiring of Helena how she liked the meal. Luckily for their hosts, the entire conversation was in German.

"The Sauerbraten, red cabbage, etc., were all excellent. The meat was of nice quality and well seasoned. I did enjoy your presentation. However, whoever made the Spaetzle, you need to send to Hinterland and have my daughter-in-law teach them how to make good Spaetzle. These things are like rubber bands." The chef turned on the tips of his toes and walked away. Hektor and Laura could have sunk into the ground. Much later they told their friends what actually had happened. The story made for a good laugh.

After almost three months in the States, it was time for Helena's return trip. Her sons often wondered if they had prevented the worst or merely delayed the inevitable.

Chapter 9

AFTER his sabbatical, Hektor started working with several interesting and challenging clients. The word had gotten around that Dr. B. was a firm believer in specialized solutions to his clients' needs; there were no two who required identical treatment.

Tonja came into Hektor's life about two years after his return from NTID. She was the third of three cousins with whom he worked in the clinic. The first, a boy, subsequently became an orally functioning child. Karlotta, his cousin, had a more severe hearing loss but nevertheless succeeded using the oral method.

He met Tonja when she was 8 months old; she was profoundly deaf. For weeks, she did nothing but scream as he held her in his arms within a soundproof environment. At last, she became used to him, the room, and the clinician assigned to her. They were able to seat her in a high chair and began teaching her using every possible means: sign, speech, amplification, graphics, touch, etc.

She was most receptive to visual input and quickly learned to absorb language through her eyes. Eventually, she was mainstreamed along with hearing as well as hearing-impaired children. At age ten or eleven, she begged her parents to allow her to be transferred to the Iowa State School for the Deaf; she wanted to become fluent in

ASL, live with deaf people, and become immersed in the culture of the deaf. She did not view herself as a handicapped person.

Looking back at his career, Hektor remembered an unforgettable moment in the life with Tonja. Her mother contacted him wanting to know if he was willing to play Santa Claus for all mainstreamed hearing-impaired children served in the local school system. At this point, he had worked with many of these kids at the clinic. Hektor agreed to be Mr. Claus for an evening. It sounded like fun. Tonja's mom had delivered a beautiful Santa outfit to his office—unbeknownst to Tonja who was not quite four years old.

Dr. B. made his appearance at the school and enjoyed seeing many of his former charges functioning and performing at their best using either speech and/or sign language. One of the boys, Harry, hopped on Santa's lap and told him in sign what he wished for Christmas. That moment was captured by a cameraman from the local newspaper, "The Hinterland Courier."

Harry and Hektor made the front page of next day's paper in living color. One of his colleagues cut out the photo and posted it on the bulletin board across from Hektor's office. A day or so later, Tonja's mom brought Hektor a beautiful fruit basket—a thank-offering from the parents of the hearing-impaired children. At the same time, Tonja's mom wanted to retrieve the neatly boxed Santa outfit. As they were chatting, Tonja walked behind Hektor's desk and took him by his hand. She marched him out of his office and started to gesture toward the picture on the bulletin board. She made sure she had his full visual attention and started to sign, pointing at the image in the picture.

"That isn't Santa Claus," she signed again and again, each time becoming more "expressive" in her communication efforts. Each of her pronouncements was followed by Hektor's reply in sign that it was indeed Santa. When she wouldn't let it go, he finally signed.

"What makes you think that isn't Santa Claus?" Her response was prompt and surprising.

"Because those are your hands!" She had only watched them for more than three years. What could he do but fess up? He told her that Santa had been so busy that he was willing to enlist him as one of his helpers. Hektor was never quite sure whether she swallowed his little white lie.

Chapter 10

THE year 1986 started most enjoyably. Albert and Margarethe at last came to visit Hektor's chosen homeland. Helena and Alex had bragged about the Midwest after their first visit in 1975. Helena couldn't say enough about her experiences in 1980 and 1981.

They finally were tempted to see for themselves. Albert and Margarethe started their month-long vacation high in the Rocky Mountains and worked their way to the Midwest. Their favorite place would always be Hideaway Park, Colorado. In time, they would experience each of the four seasons and loved them all.

Hektor taught the first half of the summer semester. He and Laura embarked on their seven-week camping trip to Alaska on the Fourth of July. Albert was quite aware of the remote locations they would be for the length of their long journey by car, ferries, and planes. They sent postcards and greetings to Helena, Albert, and Margarethe all along the way with the last one sent from the World's Fair in Vancouver, British Columbia. After seven weeks of traveling and putting seventeen thousand miles on their car, they were passing the Fraser Post Office in Colorado.

"Stop, honey. It looks like they are still open. Let me run in and get our mail. There should be tons of it." Hektor jumped out of the car.

"Let me help you with that basket. It looks heavy. I believe there is enough room on the backseat," voiced Laura. They left everything of nonimportance in the car.

"We'll take the mail in. I just want to give it a cursory glance. The unloading we can do tomorrow. I'm beat. It's been a long drive."

"Let me open all the windows. We need some fresh air in this place. It's been closed up for months," Laura announced as she walked toward the bedroom.

"This is going to feel great after sleeping in our tent for all these weeks."

"Laura, come here!" Hektor stared down at the mail basket. Toward the middle of the pile, a large white, black-rimmed envelope stood out. Hektor yanked it from the pile with one pull. He looked at the return address since he didn't recognize the writing. The letter was addressed by his nephew Alberti.

Hektor's hands began to shake. *Did Albert or Margarethe die?* He had never before received any mail from his nephew; phone calls and postcards came but never any letters. Hektor ripped open the envelope. He had to see who it was. It wasn't Albert or Margarethe; it was Helena Birken. He looked up at Laura, and she knew instantly that something had seriously gone awry.

"Laura, look at this. Mother died on August 2. My God, she has been dead and buried for fifteen days!" He shook his head in disbelief. His eyes were awash in tears. Laura walked over and gave him a firm hug. She picked up the black-rimmed envelope and looked puzzled.

"I'm so sorry for you! Oh, and look—there is a long handwritten note included." Hektor hadn't noticed it when he removed the printed death announcement from the envelope. He grasped the note and began to read out loud.

August 2, 1986

Dear Uncle Hektor, dear Aunt Laura,

I'm sorry to be the bearer of sad news. No one in the family was willing to write to you. We knew we couldn't reach you by phone. Aunt Georgine related the whole grisly story to me on the telephone the morning they found Grandma. Paula and I weren't aware of most of this stuff. You remember well how Grandmother Helena felt about me. I'll summarize what I was told by our aunt. We thought you would want to know what happened.

Aunt Georgine told me she needed to mail an important document to the tax office. Of course, she had to remind me that she had fallen on hard times after a life of luxury and wealth when Uncle Max went bankrupt. She was glad the bastard had finally died. Now, after almost thirty years of warring with her sisters, Grandmother and she had reached a truce. She kept telling me how thankful she was to Grandma for helping her find the little, inexpensive flat a couple houses up the street from her. While being glad to have a roof over her head, she detests the place and referred to her apartment as her high-rise hovel in the sky.

I had to remind her I didn't have all day to listen to her; she was calling me on my office phone. She had to go into great detail, and I wasn't prepared to listen to an operetta. Aunt Georgine finally continued her story.

She had remembered that there is a bright yellow mailbox practically in front of Grandmother's house. After depositing her letter, Aunt Georgine turned to face Grandma's apartment. She was shocked to realize what she saw; her hand had flown up to her throat and she knew something was wrong as she recalled one of the predictions by her trusted astrologer. The card reader had made similar observations.

Sorry, Uncle, you know how much stock I put in that kind of nonsense. Talk about a drama queen. Apparently, she rushed home, still huffing after her battle with the five flights of stairs, and dialed my parents' phone number. My dad barely mumbled his answer when she jumped in and told him he needed to do something about Grandma. Aunt Georgine was certain there was a problem since Grandma's shutters were still closed; and they were always up early, showing off her fancy lace curtains!

My dad reminded her that she had her own key and wanted to know why she couldn't check on her sister herself. Dad wasn't speaking with Grandma at the moment since she was angry with him and my mother for having visited you in America.

Well, you know our aunt. With her superstitions, she would never have entered Grandma's apartment alone. She chose to wait outside until my parents could get there. Rush-hour traffic apparently was pretty bad, and it took them about thirty-five minutes to arrive on the scene.

Next thing she heard was my mother screaming as she hurried down the steps, panic etched into her pale face. Aunt Georgine was anxious to learn what caused my mother's strange reaction. She and my dad found several envelopes neatly arranged on the table in Grandma's living room. My dad's and your names were written in Grandma's very distinct handwriting on two of them, but they didn't look further at the display of envelopes. Grandma wasn't in her bedroom, but then my mom found her in the bathtub. She sputtered as she related her discovery to Aunt Georgine.

Aunt Georgine, never demonstrating much faith in God, all of a sudden seemed to appeal to him and wanted to know if Grandma had drowned. Mom told her that Grandma was stark naked, but that there was no water in the tub and that they found an empty bottle of her Valium tablets lying next to her body. She was still alive.

We believe you are getting the picture. I had to stop Aunt Georgine from going on and on. Ten days later, the Almighty granted Grandmother her wish of ending her life in *Freitod*. She had at last succeeded in killing herself.

Dad knows when you are planning to be back in Winter Park. He wants to speak with you. You'll probably hear from him the night you get back to Fraser. All I will add is this. Grandma was mean to me to the bitter end. She specifically wrote she did not want "The Adenauer Bastard" and his wife attending her funeral. Do I need to say more?

We love you and feel for you!

Alberti & Paula

The letter slipped out of Hektor's hands and drifted to the carpeted floor, making barely a noise. Hektor stared at Laura.

"Can you believe this? I'm stunned."

"So am I. How could she do this to Albert, Margarethe, and the kids." The phone rang. Albert was on the line.

"You better sit down!"

"You are a bit late with that one. I'm already sitting down. Laura and I just read Alberti's letter recounting his conversation with Aunt Georgine. I'm still blown away and find it hard to accept that Mother did this to us; she finally got what she's been aiming for so many times in her troubled life."

"As you read, it was Aunt Georgine who suspected something was wrong with Mother. Those unraised jalousies were the dead giveaway. As I mentioned to Aunt Georgine when she called in hysterics, we weren't exactly on speaking terms with Mother. Once we got there, Aunt Georgine refused to go inside with us. She was certain there was something seriously wrong with our mother. The astrologer had told her most recently that some tragedy was about to occur in her immediate family. Margarethe and I searched the whole stinking apartment. That smell of garlic almost knocked us for a loop."

"I know what you mean; we had the same reaction when we were there last in '84. I don't know how her neighbors put up with it. That stench hit you in the face as soon as you entered the building. And then that bit of having to wash our hands as soon as we walked into her apartment, yelling at us not to touch anything with our 'dirty' hands. She was almost paranoid about the whole thing. I'm not sure who was kookier, Mother or Aunt Georgine with her fascination with the occult."

"You know by now, Margarethe was the one who found her in the bathtub. I'm glad for you that you didn't have to see what she looked like. We don't know what all she ingested, but whatever she took caused her body to turn pitch black wherever she came in contact with the enamel of the bathtub. Margarethe almost lost it. She was still alive when we discovered her, but she died on the second of August. In accordance with her will, she was buried next to Father on the fifth of August."

"I find it hard to believe that she demanded Alberti and Paula not attend her funeral. How can anyone be that blinded by hate? I wonder why they did an autopsy since she was alive when you found her? There must have been no question in the minds of the EMTs that she had done this to herself."

"I guess it's the law, even in a case as blatantly obvious as Mother's situation. We returned to her apartment right after we talked with the doctors at the hospital. What a horrible day! I was finally calm enough to look over all the instructions she left on the coffee table in her living room. She was clearly of sound mind and in complete control of her faculties.

"What I am trying to say is that she was sharp as a tack but also was very much troubled. I'm certain she planned this deliberately while you and Laura were in Alaska. When you read through her will and her instructions, which by now should be at the offices of your property management company, you will see what I mean. She plainly states that people's travel plans should not be interrupted with bad news."

"Are you suggesting we are responsible for her demise?"

"No, no! But Mother knew exactly what she was doing. I am also convinced she had expected Georgine to find her before Monday morning. As so often in her life, she would have celebrated another miraculous recovery. This time her plans misfired. It's very sad."

"What did the autopsy show, and what was the cause of death?"

"Thank goodness, Margarethe and I can handle blood. When the pathologist stepped away from the autopsy, he was just ripping off his bloody gloves and apron. His pronouncement was shocking to us."

"She could have lived to be a miserable one hundred. Your mother was in great physical shape. It was a blessing she died. Had she survived the ordeal, she would have been in a vegetative state for the rest of her days. It was the combination of the huge amount of arsenic and Valium that took her." Her death certificate stated that she died from poisoning after attempted suicide.

"Makes me wonder how she got that stuff. I never knew her to take Valium. But then, there are a lot of things I never knew about either of our parents; I didn't live with them all that long."

"Her will is another doozy; she is being vindictive to the bloody end. Like you, I couldn't believe her final request for Alberti and Paula not to attend her funeral. She changed her mind about certain things several times shortly before committing her deed. I can tell by all the changes she made in her handwritten document. It's all on the up and up. She had every change duly witnessed and notarized. In the end, I became her executor. I dread all that hassle. We have been through this with Margarethe's parents. I wish you were here to do this last job."

Hektor responded.

"Do you want me to take a leave? I have lots of sick days accumulated. I'm sure I can get a decent flight if I explain the circumstances."

"Thanks for offering to fly over, Hektor. There is no need for that. We have started to clear out her place. Anything of real value we moved to Werden. We are leaving everything in her bank box until you get here. Any moneys that will be left in the end are to be split evenly between the two of us. All her worldly belongings other than the dough she left to Laura, her 'favorite daughter-in-law.'"

"You're shitting me! You can't be right! No way will we stand for this; you can forget about that stipulation, last will or not. You keep those things in Germany; give some of the furnishings, china, silver, and linens, etc., to the kids if they want them. We don't want to schlepp any of that stuff back to the States. We don't know where to keep all our things now. As far as her damn "jewels" are concerned, Margarethe and Laura will evenly share the loot and pick what they want. We'll be there next spring and summer—that's when we had planned to be there anyway." Albert wasn't finished yet.

"Before I forget about it, among the treasures on the table were some of her most prized possessions. The writings and publications by Alphons von Bickel were specifically left to you. There were also photos of him and Lothar Zend. I didn't think you wanted to be reminded of that bastard after what he did to you. I took the liberty of cutting his images out of the pictures; I would have loved to castrate the real McCoy. Of course, you know what I thought of both of those guys. Last but not least, Mother left her entire library to you. If nothing else, she wants you to be sure to take the old copy of *Gone with the Wind* home to the States. She believed you treasured it all of your adult life as much as she did." Hektor could hear his brother taking a sip from his drink, which finally gave him a chance to respond to Albert.

"I am not sure if I should say thanks for the phone call. This was a real winner and deserving of sitting down. I'm going to pour myself a stiff drink and will try to digest your news. This chat will cost you a few shekels. I'll say good night. Give Margarethe and the kids hugs from both of us."

"Don't worry about the shekels. It will come off the 'inheritance heap' as Mother often called it. Remember, I'm in charge of the dough. You two sleep well. Both of you better have some of that J&B stuff you like so much. Do I dare say, good night? Talk with you soon!"

X

In early May 1987, Hektor and Laura departed for Europe. They were to meet up with dear friends at the airport in Frankfurt. Laura was glad when the jet finally lifted off from O'Hare airport. At last she found comfort in deep sleep, having taken a sleeping pill.

On their seemingly endless flight from Chicago to Frankfurt, Hektor became nostalgic, thinking about his mother's troubled life. He wasn't certain how he was going to face digging through her most personal belongings once he arrived on the scene almost a year after her death. The many letters and photographs collected through seventy-nine years of living would be staring back at him, reminders of the countless, well-known circumstances during Helena's earthly sojourn.

Hektor sipped his drink. He sobbed, pressing a handkerchief to his face. *Mother, I wish you had committed the story of your life to paper in your inimitable handwriting, documenting the most poignant events in your tragic existence. Did you expect me to tell your tale, knowing that I still have every one of the hundreds of letters you wrote to me over the course of more than forty-three years? How vividly I remember you sharing with me all that happened in your life.* Hektor leaned back in his comfortable seat, recalling the troubled days on earth of Helena Krämer Birken.

"I was born in 1907, the Krämers' first child. Although my young parents were somewhat disappointed that their offspring was not male and able to carry on the family name, they accepted me and loved me in their own way.

"As I grew into a toddler, I had a healthy crop of dark hair. And as it was the fashion, my hair was always adorned with a gigantic bow attached on the left side. By the time I was four and had been joined by a brother and sister, my mother noticed that I had the tendency to appear cross-eyed. Your grandmother consulted an eye doctor, only to learn that the condition was made worse by the ever-present large bow. The object of adornment was promptly abandoned, and I wore a patch to strengthen my eye muscles. The condition was largely corrected although I retained the lazy-eye phenomenon for the rest of my life when I was under excessive strain, as you well remember.

"Reportedly, my mother found herself with child regularly; however, only three children survived during their first eight years of marriage. Arthur, my one and only brother, was born in 1909, and my sister, Elsa, came along in 1911. At the time of my father's induction into the military in 1915, my mother had to deal with a successful business and tend to three growing children.

"Although small of stature, I was expected to assume certain responsibilities around the household and the shop. While Grandma always had adequate help tending to many facets of running her house and business, she made sure that I did not occupy myself too deeply with child's play. Even an eight-year-old had to make some contribution to the war effort. In that respect, my parents acted not much differently from the norm. No one had yet heard of child labor laws in those years. It was common practice to put children to work and make them useful as soon as they were capable of making some sort of contribution to the cause.

"My teachers often thought I was a precocious child with an exceptional memory for detail. Already in my early school years, it was often pointed out to my mother that I appeared to be particularly gifted in reading, writing, and arithmetic. While I was never especially artistic, in time I became accomplished at playing the piano.

"It was just past my eighth birthday when my father was suddenly taken into the army. How well I remember father emptying the large safe in the tiny anteroom that served as a warming hut for the help in the butcher shop during the depth of winter.

"I can still see him piling all those gold coins on the large, round, pedestal table. It almost seemed like it was going to give way under the weight of the stacked gold pieces. He told us kids to take a good look at all that gold because it would never be in use again at the end of the damn war. Arthur and Elsa were too young to comprehend what Father was saying. I rarely liked speaking of the ensuing war years and how they affected me and my family.

"Father was gone for three years with the exception of one short furlough towards the very end of the disastrous war. Later people called it the 'Great War'; I never could conceive of any war as being great. In my mind, wars were fought to enrich industrialists and to sacrifice the sons of ordinary people for cannon fodder. Those of wealth and power rarely gave their sons for any cause.

"Your grandfather returned from the war in 1918 and found his family intact. While we had learned to live on little, none of us starved, as had so many Germans during the latter part of the war. It was often said that defeat came as a result of the terrible depression, starvation, and pestilence suffered by those behind the front. Our house survived World War I, and the business was still a going concern—although on an extremely limited scale.

"The big surprise during the post-war era was the birth of my youngest sister. Georgine was born in December 1919. Your grandparents would look upon her as their song of joy in their years of retirement and old age.

"In 1920, right after the holidays, there was a phone call from our family physician. My parents learned that I contracted tuberculosis, and I was sent to a small sanitarium in Davos, Switzerland. A year later, I returned to the family fold, my body apparently healed. The impact of the much-feared illness was always on my mind. As you well know, I constantly worried about passing the disease on to you boys.

"I returned to the Luisenschule, the *Gymnasium* for girls. My teachers continued to advise my parents that I was exceptionally gifted. Everyone recognized this fact except my father who rejected the idea of women studying at a university, a place strictly and exclusively appropriate for males.

"By the time I was older, I was often asked to take phone orders in the flourishing trade. I was seventeen when I learned the hard way that it was best to address certain persons in the manner which they desired. On one occasion, I was taking an order for a 'Frau Major Sachs' but insisted on simply calling her 'Frau Sachs.'

"'Young lady, did you not catch my proper name? It is Frau Major Sachs.'

"'Yes, Frau Sachs. What else may we have ready for pickup when your chauffeur stops by tomorrow?'

"'The impertinence!' Frau Sachs exclaimed. 'I will take this up with Herr Krämer tomorrow. For now, that is all,' and she replaced the receiver.

"I shrugged, feeling good that I had not stooped to that person's level of arrogance. As promised, Mrs. Sachs took up the matter with your grandfather. She made her grand entrance into the store followed by her chauffeur.

"'I demand to speak with Herr Krämer. I have a serious complaint to level against the young woman who took my order over the phone yesterday. I believe it was the eldest daughter.'

"My mother asked one of the clerks to summon Father from the butcher's kitchen. As he emerged, obviously heated and not particularly pleased to be interrupted, he was tying a sparkling white apron over one that had clearly been bloodied by what he was doing. No introductions were necessary. The astute businessman he was, he addressed the woman properly."

"'What can I do for you, Frau Major Sachs? Did you have a problem with any of our products you purchased?'

"'With the quality of your products, never. However, the person who took my order yesterday failed to address me properly in spite of my repeated demands to be called by my rightful title. Obviously, you know it.'

"'Who took the order for Frau Major Sachs yesterday?' barked my father. Of course, it was I, and I was summoned promptly.

"'Did you take the order for Frau Major Sachs? What seems to be the problem with calling the lady by her proper title?' Father insisted.

"I said, 'I'm so sorry, but I didn't know that was necessary. After all, she isn't the major; her husband is. People don't call my mother *Frau Corporal Krämer*! I had to control myself to keep from laughing into the woman's face.'

"'You apologize to Frau Major Sachs, this minute. In the future, you will address our patrons by their titles. You and I will have a little chat later, young lady,' said my father.

"I proceeded with my apology, albeit not exactly genuflecting as might have been expected of me. Frau Major Sachs instructed the chauffeur to carry the packages after she advised my mother to put the amount due on her running tab. She turned to leave, making her exit with a definite flourish.

"I was too old to receive a whipping, and deep down in his heart, Father shared my opinion of the snobbish bitch. Nevertheless, he let me know that he never wanted to be confronted again by an unhappy and insulted patron. And that was it. As so often in life, I had no problem speaking out against people who rubbed me the wrong way. It was often said that I had the touch of a revolutionary in me."

Hektor couldn't help stifling a good laugh when he recalled his mother telling the story of the school for scandal with her inimitable bravura. It was an event Helena never forgot.

"I was eighteen when Mother believed it was high time for me to be sent to a finishing school. After perusing all sorts of professional journals, Mother settled on the School of Refinement for Young Ladies in Schmalkalden, Thuringia, an area of Germany totally foreign to her and my father. Nevertheless, they were impressed by the advertisement and contacted the school.

"My father studied the contract to be signed, and after his careful reading, opted to insert a clause, allowing me to leave the place after a six-week probationary period if I was unhappy with the school for any reason. Madame von Schnickel and her son, an attorney, accepted the amended contract. Soon I was on my way to Schmalkalden.

"When I departed with several suitcases and hat boxes, one of the suitcases was filled with wonderful salamis, cheeses, and good bread. My father insisted I be prepared in case I would not be fed decent food in that distant place.

"Arriving at the train station in Schmalkalden, I was picked up by Madame von Schnickel and her son with a chauffeur-driven limousine. On the way, they stopped at an upscale delicatessen and bought an impressive assortment of cold cuts, meats, and cheeses.

"When partaking of the first meal at the elegant residence, I discovered that the other seventeen students and I were served nothing but the cheapest of cold cuts and mystery meats on stale bread, prompting my inquiry.

"'What happened to all the stuff you bought this morning?'

"'You are here to learn and not to be indulged. In the next few days, you will have an opportunity to serve me delicacies in a proper manner. Today, you will practice clearing the table and learn how to properly wash our finest Meissen porcelain.'

"The snooty son mumbled in response to his mother: 'We've got ourselves a revolutionary!'

"I got up from the table and stormed up to my room which I was sharing with two other young ladies, Herta Weinbrand and Gertrude Nimmersatt. As soon as Gertrude walked into the room, she lived up to her name, 'Never Satiated.'

"'Do I smell food in one of those suitcases?'

"I wound up sharing my treasured hoard with the other seventeen girls; they had been starved for a decent sandwich. Herta got into the act.

"'Just wait until you have to play Molly Mop for these pompous asses; I'm up for that duty next week when those two spend the morning at the spa and shopping.'

"'Be careful when you dust that bastard's office and don't disturb anything in his safe; last time I dusted, I noticed the door to his safe was ajar,' mumbled Gertrude.

"That's all Herta had to hear. She couldn't wait to get into that office and check out the safe. When she got the office assignment, she couldn't believe her good fortune; the safe was indeed open. She laid hands on Gertrude's, a couple of other close friends', and my files and removed them. She took the contracts straight to the incinerator and gave the pocket money our captors were holding to each of the respective 'prisoners.'

"'Tomorrow, when they are resting their useless, fat bodies, we are out of here and on our way home,' announced Herta.

"Herta would let her father's corporate lawyers worry about the aftermath as she shouted: *'Après moi le déluge!'* [No matter what comes!]

"Herta ordered a large cab to haul us and all our belongings to the train station. By the time Madame von Schnickel and her son learned of the well-planned breakout, we were on our way. We took the first train heading south to get out of town quickly. It was always possible to buy a connecting ticket to our respective hometowns on the train.

"As soon as they discovered who had escaped, Herr Doctor headed for his office, only to discover the unlocked safe and the missing contracts and pocket money. He and his mother were of one opinion it was the 'revolutionary' who had incited the other girls. Within hours, he posted a registered letter to my parents, threatening to take me and my family to court. A similar letter was posted to the parents of the other four girls who escaped. My father was concerned as he addressed me.

"'That isn't the end of it. I'm sure we will hear from Herr Doctor von Schnickel in short order. In a way, I am sorry that you didn't stay your six weeks and then come home. However, from what you told me, I can't blame you or your compatriots. I presume you have Herta Weinbrand's address since she was the instigator of this whole affair?'

"Oh, yes, Father, we intend to stay in touch."

"My father contacted Herr Weinbrand, and they agreed to meet fire with fire. Herta's parents were just as infuriated as mine when they learned of the predicaments in which we found ourselves.

"'If the von Schnickels threaten to sue, I will have one of my attorneys get in touch with them. I will place advertisements in every professional journal the von Schnickels use to ensnare parents like us. We need to discourage others from providing these people with slave labor at dear prices to their well-meaning parents. That will put a quick stop to their enterprise. Let's wait and see what happens,' was Herta's father's assessment.

"Sure enough, all involved parents received registered letters post haste; each contained a similar threat of legal action by Herr Doctor von Schnickel. Herta's father and attorneys fired the promised opening salvo. Not only did they proceed with the ad campaign, but countersued. In the absence of any legal documentation and we girls only too willing to testify against our former oppressors, Herr von Schnickel backed off in a hurry. Their prosperous but scandalous School of Refinement for Young Ladies went out of business in short order."

Hektor couldn't help himself; he laughed out loud, feeling guilty to disturb other passengers who were sleeping.

"What's so funny?" inquired the kind stewardess as she leaned down to Hektor. "Would you care for another drink?"

"I certainly would! I just relived a couple of funny episodes in the life of my departed mother; it only happened sixty-two years ago." Miss Pan American smiled as she handed Hektor his J&B on lots of ice. For a moment, he closed his eyes as his thoughts turned back to the life of his mother.

"I attended a finishing school in Swabia in 1926. The school, Stiftsgrundhof, outside of Stuttgart, was run largely by an order of Protestant sisters. That experience was the happiest in my young life. What clouded this joy-filled year was my discovery of a book called *Mein Kampf* by Adolf Hitler. I learned of its publication the year before and knew that the author was associated with the hooligans who recently had caused so many problems in big cities.

"I read the book every chance I had. I abhorred the ideas presented by the author and became concerned for the many Jewish friends of my family. The more I learned, the more I knew this was not the direction in which the country should be moving. I made up my mind that I would do anything to challenge such disturbing ideas. I considered what the Nazis might do to Herta and her family. My visions literally made me sick to my stomach. I don't know how often I wondered what could happen to my new friend.

"All employees working for my family were housed in the five-story building erected in 1906. In 1928, Alex, your father, a young journeyman, joined the ever-growing number of employees at the butcher shop. Your father had lost his mother in 1925 and his father in 1927. Quite often my father caught me speaking to, perhaps flirting with, young Alex and was pleased that I seemed to take a curious interest in your father. Your grandfather immediately began looking at your father as a prospective son-in-law.

"Your Vati and I were married on Christmas Day of 1930. Your grandfather insisted on a quick marriage to salvage what was left of your father's poorly managed and drained parental inheritance. I worked like a slave from the day I set foot on the property in Düsseldorf; but no matter how hard I tried, the hotel business was doomed to failure. We went bankrupt in 1937. Your father, you, Albert, and I returned to Essen.

"Within days of my return to my hometown, I became successful at running a branch for one of my father's competitors. Unlike your father, I enjoyed the taste of success. I thrived on hard work and being in control of my own fate. Your father tried being a salesman; he was a dismal failure. When the induction notice arrived, it was a welcome relief from a job he found distasteful. Both he and I had been raised in environments of affluence. The difference was that I could rise from the ashes of defeat and your father could not. He longed for the days of comfort with his parents and simply could not cope with the fact that he had to get up in the morning and work for someone else.

"In 1938, the opportunity presented itself for your father and me to open our own business. By the time your father marched off to war, I had conquered the neighborhood and had a firm foothold among competitors in the area. I had a gift of gab and could sell anything.

"I learned to drive and bought my first car, a little Steyr. At age thirty-four, I was an attractive woman. I had a trim figure and wore my thick, dark brunette hair in the fashionable upswept style that was the rage during World War II. I was a voracious reader and garnered a copy of *Gone with the Wind* before its publication was forbidden. I loved the feisty character of Scarlett O'Hara, whose famous slogans I made my own.

"Herta Weinbrand and I remained staunch friends until Herta and her parents escaped to Casablanca in 1938. In the first and last letter I received from Casablanca, ninety percent or more of the writing was blackened by the authorities. It rendered the letter useless. Sadly, I never heard from Herta again.

"After your father's furlough in 1941, I discovered much to my dismay that I was pregnant. You were with me when I had the accident on the street car. The child was stillborn in early 1942. I mourned the loss of a third boy, but I had to move on with my life. There were so many challenges in my busy days.

"It was well known by friends and family that I was adamantly opposed to the Nazi regime and often took issue with those who tried to control my fate. I was fortunate that the Nazis never put me in a concentration camp.

"I took everything in stride: Your father's injury in Russia and confinement in a hospital in Baden-Baden, the separation from you boys whom I had to send to southern Germany, numerous confrontations with Nazi officials, the many bomb attacks on the city of Essen, the countless horrors of war, and the trauma of postwar Germany. I mourned the loss of my only brother and three cousins to whom I was very close."

"Darling, you are snoring. I'm sorry to disturb you, but it is time for you to wake up anyway. The stewardess didn't have the heart to stir you for breakfast. She told me about the number of drinks you had and reliving some of your mother's escapades. Why didn't you waken me and talk to me instead of dealing with your concerns on your own?"

"I was glad you could sleep. You know me and long-distance flights and sleeping on airplanes. It just doesn't work for me. I suppose I should have tried a stiff drink and one of your sleeping pills; that might have done it for me. Well, I spent the night with Helena."

"It's good you didn't try the combination of pills and booze; that could have done you in!"

Hektor and Laura settled in for seven weeks in Europe. They traveled with good friends for the first three weeks and finally arrived in Essen. Hektor was pleased to show his friends some of the high points in southern Germany and the Alpine countries. They ended their tour with a stop in Köndringen. Aunt Klara was overjoyed to meet their friends and to spend a few days with Hektor and Laura. Subconsciously, Hektor must have wanted to delay dealing with his mother's untimely death for as long as possible.

Almost a year passed before Hektor faced the grim reality of his mother's death. Helena would miss so many things that should have given her much joy. Within a year after her self-execution, a great-granddaughter was born. Jessica, a sister to Jutta, would be born eighteen months later. Helena's badly timed death was such a waste.

After their arrival in Essen, Hektor and Laura visited Aunt Georgine, Helena's youngest sibling. Georgine's telling of a final story involving her older sister made them smile; it made them forget momentarily the sad situation they had to face.

"You heard your mother didn't want certain people at her funeral. She was very specific about this. The few of us who attended the wake gathered at Birkenhains. You remember the old Gaststätte near the Parkfriedhof, don't you? We were all telling stories about your mother. Some were really funny. Anyway, suddenly this large piece of plaster broke away from the ceiling. It descended upon us, particularly me. I ducked and was merely grazed by the plaster on my right shoulder. Of course, you know how superstitious I am. I just knew it was your mother's ghost haunting us. I lifted my glass toward the ceiling.

"Prost, Helena!" [To your health, Helena]. Everyone chuckled at that.

"After my toast, she left us alone." Hektor and Laura couldn't help laughing; it was so Aunt Georgine.

Hektor eventually dealt with the sad reality of digging his

way through many of his mother's personal belongings. He leafed through Alphons von Bickel's collections of poetry and read some of their personal letters. He did not consider them "drivel," contrary to Lothar Zend's hateful assessment of their correspondence forty some years ago. Hektor was hoping that miserable bastard had died a painful death.

The poetry and writings were indeed reflective of Alphons and Helena's appreciation of expression in the German language. Their discussions concerning prominent writers in German literature, the great minds of their time and in the past, and their total disenchantment with the leadership of the Third Reich were profound. Lothar Zend was correct in one pronouncement. Alphons and Helena's relationship was strictly platonic. They clearly admired each other and appreciated the same things in life. They functioned on a high intellectual plateau. Hektor still had a hard time dealing with the relationship between Lothar and Alphons that might have existed in their younger years.

Turning the pages in Helena's morning and evening readings, he found countless clippings of poetry that obviously meant much to her. Many of these were "dark" in content and often dealt with death. Sitting there among her most personal possessions and sorting through years and years of evidence of a life in constant emotional turmoil, Hektor broke down and cried.

When he was a young boy, he absolutely loved his mother without reservation. She had been his support and shield against the forces of the outside world. He admired her courage and wanted to emulate her later in life. As he grew older, theirs became a love-hate relationship. Hektor had much difficulty in dealing with Helena's indescribable jealousy, vindictiveness, narrow-mindedness, and intolerance of persons professing faiths other than Protestantism.

Hektor at last had seen it all. It was such a wasted life; such a sad ending. She deserved better than this. Most of her life was a struggle. Helena never really had it easy—not as a child and not as an adult. Her frequent attempts at gaining freedom in death were cries for help that were ignored by those around her or were misunderstood. Family and society weren't ready or willing to recognize her as being manic depressive. The stigma on the family was too great. Much could have been done to address Helena's illness. The time wasn't ripe for finding and applying the needed means to rescue her from her emotional abyss.

I can't look anymore at the evidence of your troubled life. I wish you hadn't done this to us. Why did you have to kill yourself? He walked up the many steps to the third floor of Albert and Margarethe's building. He faced his brother.

"Pour me a triple J&B, please." Albert handed him the glass.

"That bad, eh?" Hektor didn't say a word and walked out on the balcony and listened to the church bells ringing. He was clutching Greta's silver Madonna in his left hand. If Helena's spirit was among them, Hektor knew his mother would not be pleased. He didn't care. Deep emotions welled up in his chest. He freely shed the tears he had wanted to shed so often in the last few months. He openly sobbed. Hektor didn't care who heard or saw him. He lifted his glass toward the church steeple as the bells proclaimed eventide.

"Here's to you, Mother; here's to a courageous life lived; here's to a death—undeserved!"

Chapter 11

THEIR phone rang after one o'clock in the morning on February 23, 1991. Hektor picked up the receiver, totally annoyed as he glanced at the clock and realized what time it was.

"Who the hell is calling at this hour?"

"Hi, Hektor, it's Elaine." He could tell she was crying.

"I'm sorry, honey. I thought it was another one of those damn calls we get from the nursing home at all hours of the night. I'm beginning to hate that job of your sister's. What's wrong? I can tell you are terribly upset."

"We just had a phone call from Duluth. Monty had a terrible accident. He fell down twelve concrete steps and was badly injured. We don't know all the details yet, but he was taken by ambulance to the trauma center. We don't know how fast we can get there. Margo is at a swim meet in Stevens Point. She and Gunner will be on their way up there as soon as Gunner can get to Eau Claire. Can you and Laura meet them at the hospital in Duluth?"

"Of course we can. We'll be on our way as soon as we get some clothes on. We are so sorry to hear this. We'll be in touch. Love you."

⋈

Laura was still in a stupor.

"That was Elaine; Monty has been in a devastating accident in Duluth. Let's get a few things packed and be on our way. Elaine and Charles have no idea how fast they can get there from San Diego. Margo and Gunner are heading up to Duluth now."

Laura and Hektor were dressed and ready to go in minutes. They made sure they wore warm and practical things, not knowing what kind of weather they might run into. It was one forty in the morning when Hektor backed the car out of the garage in Hinterland. He looked at Laura, who was softly crying.

"I don't know what possessed me to get gas last night. We ought to be OK until we get to Duluth. Depending on how things go, I might tank up again in Minneapolis as we zip through the city. Did you by any chance pay attention to the weather report last night? I didn't."

"No. I was so tired when I came home; I hardly felt like eating, never mind watching what was going on in the world. We can't worry about it. Let's just hope for the best. We'll keep the radio on and find a local weather station as we get closer."

Hektor turned the radio on, seeking some distraction in pleasant music. Neither said very much. They were both off in their own worlds thinking about Monty. Laura spoke at last, not knowing yet how serious Monty's injuries were.

"It's almost like his whole life is flashing through my mind. You know I always thought he and Margo were the kids we never could have. We were so fortunate that Elaine and Charles allowed us to be involved with their children and spend as much time with them as we did. I can still see that towhead fearlessly jumping into the pool in Newport News or visiting the Marine Museum with us a year later, commenting on all the 'boats'—speaking as clearly as a bell.

"I loved having him ski with us for the week during our spring break in 1983. He was so much fun, and what a wonderful and accomplished skier he was. I'm so glad we could be there for his confirmation and the graduation parties and everything else we did together. I so enjoyed working with him to get ready for Margo's graduation events. He had outgrown his teenage pains and become such a pleasant young man to be with. I cannot imagine anything bad happening to him. From what you told me, Elaine was very concerned. I can't wait for us to get there," voiced Laura softly between sniffling and breathing hard. They made it to Minneapolis in less than four hours and were through the city before morning traffic. It also helped that it was a Saturday. They literally raced through downtown Minneapolis.

"I think it's uncanny that there are never any patrol cars lurking in the dark when you are hoping they'll come to your aid and get you more quickly to your destination. I don't know how often I have wished for a police escort to expedite matters. No such luck this time around, I guess." The roads were dry until seventy miles south of Duluth, when it began snowing steadily.

"I'd hoped we didn't have to deal with this stuff. Let's pray we make it before things really get bad," mumbled Hektor.

Laura had dozed off. Despite roads becoming snow covered, they made it in six hours from Hinterland to Duluth without stopping for anything. They were greeted by Margo and Gunner, his mother, and some of their friends. Margo hugged them and started to cry.

"Monty isn't doing well at all. These doctors tell us that he is gone for all intents and purposes. They keep saying his brain was totally destroyed. You know what that means."

"Let me see what else we can learn. I'll speak to the attending physicians." Margo introduced Hektor as her uncle, Dr. Hektor Birken, to the young doctors attending Monty.

"Please come over here and look at these scans. We are sure you are acquainted with the format. As you can see, the area of his brain stem was totally destroyed and the profuse bleeding has spread the damage into pretty much the entire cortex. All testing we have done so far confirms total absence of any cortical activity. He has been given massive drug infusions to reduce the pressure on the brain." Hektor could clearly see the extent of the impact.

"None of us here can make any decisions; you must wait for the arrival of our nephew's parents. They are trying to get here from San Diego. We expect them to arrive later this afternoon." A third doctor came on the scene and became terribly annoying.

"The young man's driver's license indicates his willingness to be an organ donor. We should harvest his organs now before they become totally useless." Hektor almost lost it.

"If I hear you use that terminology one more time, I will report you to the ethics board of this hospital. And furthermore, if there is any organ donation to be considered, it will be at the discretion of his parents."

Hektor had to walk away from the jerk before he really let him have it. As the hours slipped by, more and more of Monty's friends said farewell to their fallen hero. None of the family had any idea how many friends Monty actually had. It was a long day of waiting for Elaine and Charles to arrive from San Diego. They managed to transfer to the last flight leaving the snowed-in Minneapolis airport. The plane barely made the landing in Duluth. Finally, shortly after five o'clock in the afternoon, they were with them. A team of physicians consulted with Elaine and Charles and immediate members of the family.

"As you can see in these images, Monty's brain is completely destroyed. Our tests show absolutely no cortical activity. We recommend that he be taken off life support. However, before we can do that, we have to take him off all medications and run another battery of tests to confirm the absence of any brain-wave activity. Then, and only then, will he be taken off life support. Do all of you understand what we are saying?"

Elaine and Charles just nodded. They were numb. None could fully grasp what was happening; it was all surreal and yet steeped in the utter starkness of reality. They walked out of the examining room and made weak attempts at consoling each other. By now, Millie Prior, Caitlin, and her husband had arrived from Detroit.

)𝕏(

The test results were shared with the family early on Monday morning. The "harvesting man" stood in the back. Hektor would have hit him had he used that line one more time. If looks could have killed, the bastard would have been dead as far as Hektor was concerned. One of the other doctors addressed the family.

"The latest test battery confirms once again that there is no longer any cortical activity. Let me show you the graphs. Monty could continue to live for quite a while with the life support that has sustained him, but he would always remain in a vegetative state. As hard as this may sound to all of you, it would be kind and humane to this beautiful young man if you would allow him to go to his Maker now. Listening to his young friends and all of you, I believe this is what he would want you to do." All nodded in agreement with what they were told.

"In accordance with your consent, we will proceed with taking Monty off life support. We will leave you alone for a few moments, allowing you to say goodbye to your dear boy."

Medical personnel backed out of the room and left the family standing with Monty. They formed a circle by holding his hands and spoke a prayer. One by one they touched and kissed Monty's beautiful face and made their farewells. Margo nearly collapsed.

"I never wanted to be an only child. Why do you need to leave us?"

It further broke everyone's hearts. They shrouded Monty with their love and were certain his spirit was among them. They almost felt like they were playing the role of God by having made the decision to let him go.

Monty's funeral was a testimonial to his popularity among his contemporaries and adults. The family was aware of many of his friends but never realized how many hundreds of other lives he had touched in his brief sojourn on earth. Randolph, one of his closest buddies, tucked a photo into a pocket of Monty's suit before he kissed his friend goodbye. There were few eyes in the room that didn't reflect the anguish all were suffering.

In the weeks following Monty's tragic death, Hektor had his moments. Sometimes just looking at a young student or even a child who reminded him of Monty would trigger an emotional breakdown. Letting Monty go was the hardest thing he did in his life including the aftermath of an ugly divorce, the separation from his own children, and the death of grandparents and parents. Hektor's hair turned completely white within a matter of weeks.

The tragedy confirmed for all that they simply lived too far apart. While the phone helped them to stay in touch, all lived from one occasion to the next until they could reach out to each other's comforting arms. Elaine and Charles made countless trips back to the Midwest to be with Margo, their close friends in Minnesota, and Hektor and Laura. On the occasion of Charles and Elaine's twenty-fifth anniversary, they laughed and cried a lot while trying to recall happier days.

Initially, none of them wanted to do anything traditional, including being home. In the end, Charles and Elaine wanted to be with family rather than in some hotel at a strange and distant place. In spite of terrible traveling conditions on both Thanksgiving and Christmas, they were all content to be at the Birken home in Hinterland. They chose these gatherings as times for renewal, as times to look toward new beginnings. None of them, whose lives Monty had touched, would ever be the same; but Monty would have wanted them to move on and to look toward new horizons because he was such a lover of life. As they prepared themselves for the arrival of 1992, they kept these sentiments hidden deep in their inner selves.

Epilogue

More than thirty years have passed since Helena died. A great many of Hektor and Laura's good friends and family members have joined her on that last journey. Monty has already been gone for twenty-eight years. Recently, Hektor reflected on his own life and on those who had such a profound impact on his existence.

There was his mother, Helena Birken. He admired her courage in the face of adversity, but he didn't share her strong convictions regarding faith and other aspects of life. He still could not believe how she treated her one and only grandchild in Germany. Hektor had long forgiven her the deed of seeking freedom from an extremely unhappy life but could never forget that she had done it. He remembered her love for him as a very young boy but also could not forgive her the hate and jealousy she harbored for some of his most beloved and honored friends and relatives. He would always be thankful to her for endowing him with her thirst for knowledge as well as her abundant love for language.

His father, Alex Birken, was a real Mensch. He opened Hektor's eyes to a lifelong appreciation of classical music and the world of opera. Looking back, he really didn't know his father for very long. He couldn't recall any special moments when he was a little boy.

His interactions were framed by a mere ten years before Hektor embarked on a distant life in the New World.

Aunt Klara took care of Albert and him during World War II in the little village of Köndringen. She blessed him with the happiest years of his childhood. He always felt welcome as he returned to her loving and open arms whenever he and Laura paid her a visit during the course of many years.

His aunts were all so different. Aunt Marianne, his father's only sibling, was the epitome of kindness and gentility. She was soft-spoken and delighted whenever Hektor called on her. Aunt Marianne understood why his marriage to Georgia turned into a major disaster.

His mother's youngest sister, Georgine, charmed everyone with her wit and biting tongue; she loved living in the fast lane. She was well-known for her beliefs in the occult and mysterious. As much of a gambler as she was, she never went to any casino unless her tarot cards or trusted astrologer had conveyed the right signals. Her superstitions were the stuff of legend.

Aunt Elsa was elegant, stylish, and had a flair for living; she taught Hektor to dance before he took formal lessons at Dartmund's Emporium of Dance. He always regretted that she and Helena could not forgive and forget their trials and tribulations after Grandfather Krämer passed away. The family discord left Hektor extremely shaken.

Aunt Georgine's first husband, Franz Dimmelsburg, was the son-in-law who played such an important part in the fortunes of the Krämers. He, too, passed on much too early, leaving his young son, Markus, to fend for himself under the tutelage of a stepfather who turned out to be a fortune hunter and crook par excellence. He left Hektor with very few positive memories.

There were his teachers: Krantopf, Nagelmann, Wagemann, and Korsch. All of them profoundly affected and shaped his early education in Germany. If it hadn't been for them, he probably would never have immigrated to the United States; the thought would not have crossed his mind.

His school chum and friend Nicklaus Beerenbaum showed him how to enjoy life and introduced Hektor to his parents, Greta and Kurt Beerenbaum, and his sister, Judith. In time, the Beerenbaums became his adoptive family.

Greta Beerenbaum allowed him a glimpse into a world of affluence and glamor and, even more so, into a loving family environment. Greta bestowed on him the gift of the silver Madonna, which protected him throughout his adult life. She fell in love with Laura from the moment they met; their friendship endured until the day she died. Her death came suddenly and unexpectedly; Hektor often wondered if she had become tired of living.

Kurt Beerenbaum was his mentor and the "second father" who afforded him entrée into social circles he had never dreamt of. He loved him for opening his eyes to the wonders of winter and downhill skiing. Sadly, he also died much too young. His death forever changed the lives of Greta and her children.

His friend Peter Weldenfeldt and his family welcomed him into their lives. Like the Beerenbaums, they opened Hektor's eyes to a world of glamor and well-being. While they wished him the best in his adventures of wanting to explore the New World, they assured him they were willing to play a major role in his professional life if he chose to return to Germany.

Hannah and Werner von Unselm, his American sponsors, afforded him the opportunity to discover the New World, although their failure to share the dilemmas of their own lives prevented Hektor from altering his plans of experiencing the New World. Had he been aware of their impending divorce, he probably would not have left Germany. Unwittingly, they impacted his entire life.

Doretta Osram, Hektor's first love and fiancée, fell victim to the scheming of his future first wife. He often recalled their final meeting in Zurich. The alleged tragic disappearance from this earth of her and her family saddened him greatly.

His longest-standing American friends, Estelle and Patrick Swansong, Gertrude and Knut Schiefer, Marietta and Burton Eppelrath, and Martina Parcells, stood by him during the darkest days of his early years in New York. He could never forget the vital roles they played in his decision to seek new beginnings after four disastrous years of living with Georgia.

Georgia Unkovsky, his first wife, ensnared him and forever changed the course of his life. Unintended, through her maneuvers, she may have saved his life by insisting he not sail back to New York on the ill-fated *Andrea Doria*. Hektor chose to believe that a Greater Being had served him well.

Dr. Schweikert opened his eyes to serious problems in Hektor's relationship with his first wife, Georgia.

Crusty Harry Rundstadt actually rescued him from the Atlantic during the most dismal days of his failed marriage to Georgia and remained one of his staunchest friends throughout his life. Hektor and Harry were linked serendipitously, but their friendship endured many a storm in their personal lives in the years that followed.

Harry's parents, Adelaide Gertrude and Harry, Sr., always remained dear to Hektor.

His German friends, Walter and Else Gunders, stood by him; Else was a remarkable woman—some called her a steel magnolia.

Dave Mandelbaum finally brought closure to his legal battles with Georgia; Hektor gained his freedom but for many years lost touch with his children, Frank and Karen.

The untimely death of his housemate, Lew Simons, in Cleveland caused Hektor to be transferred to Detroit; serendipity once again changed the direction his life would take.

Robert and Lora Mitchell kept Hektor on an even keel during his first years in Detroit.

There were Bob Henkel and his friend Deena, who arranged *the* blind date with his future wife, Laura—Hektor's love and friend for a lifetime.

The many professors and persons during his eight years of studying at Wayne State University shall remain unnamed.

Likewise unnamed are the colleagues, students, and clients who crossed his path during his twenty-five years in Hinterland.

The Visions Lodge hosts, Nora and Larry, introduced Hektor and Laura to the magic of Hideaway Park and allowed them to give flight to their personal Phoenix.

In adulthood, Hektor learned to appreciate his brother, Albert, and his endearing wife, Margarethe, as well as his nephew, Albert, Jr., and Albert's wife, Paula. Their daughters, Jutta and Jessica, became key players in Hektor and Laura's lives.

And there was Mom, Millie Prior, Laura's mother, one of his most faithful supporters—especially in his educational quests during the prime of his life.

Caitlin, Laura's youngest sister, could make him chuckle. Her beloved Valentino, her hundred-pounds-of-love golden doodle, became Hektor and Laura's late-in-life child after Caitlin's untimely passing. They called each other Zachariah and Elisabeth.

Last but not least, Laura's sister, Elaine; Charles Angenous, her husband; and their very special children, Monty and Margo, were Hektor's American family in every way. Monty's tragic death in 1991 touched Hektor and everyone in the family deeply. Margo and her husband, Gunner, blessed the family with David, Colleen, and Trevor.

✕

Hideaway Park had been seen as their final domicile in life. It was Hektor and Laura's dream when they were younger. Alas, eight months of winter became a burden. In late March of 2003, they were on their way to the sunny Southwest and learned that their hideaway was "blessed" with more than eight feet of new snow (atop the five or more feet already on the ground) in less than forty-eight hours. Hektor concluded enough was enough.

They arrived in Arizona on a Monday night and signed a contract to build a new house two days later. Hektor's resolve to bid farewell to their mountain home and explore the wonders of the American Southwest almost put Laura into catatonic shock.

"I can't believe you are doing this to us. How many times have you told me you would never live in the South? How much further south than Arizona can you get? We will practically live in Mexico; it is only thirty-five miles from where you wish to live. What are we going to do with two big houses? What if the house in Colorado doesn't sell right away?"

"Stop worrying, Laura. The worst that can happen, we will have a mortgage on the new house. Thank God, our present home is paid for." He could have shot the designer with whom they met to discuss all necessities for finishing the new house.

"You'll get used to rattlesnakes, herds of javelinas, scorpions, Gila monsters, tarantulas, bugs that are big enough to carry a saddle, hundred-degree-plus days of summer, and the fact that most things that grow here 'bite' you." That was all Laura needed to hear. She almost made Hektor back out of the deal while they still could.

The mountain home was sold three days after their return. They sold it without benefit of a realtor. Six months later, the moving van pulled up in Arizona. They arrived at their new home after a challenging summer of building a house from one thousand miles away. They became involved in the community and found their respective niches. Hektor pursued a fourth career in the worlds of art and writing and discovered that there was indeed life after academia.

Estranged from his children, Frank and Karen, for more than thirteen years, they learned of Frank's devastating accident early in 2003. Frank awoke from a three-month coma and was left brain-damaged. Through the modern miracle of technology, Hektor and Laura stayed in touch with the children and eventually established a more amicable relationship. At the time of Frank's first serious accident, Hektor learned that their mother, Georgia, had passed away six years earlier. Regular visits to the East Coast became the rule and brought them closer to Frank, Karen, and their families.

⚭

Turning the corner of age seventy, Hektor believed it was time to fulfill his life-long dream of seeing the world. Often he recalled the final scene in the movie "Auntie Mame." Rosalind Russell, all decked out in a stunning sari, ascended a sweeping stairway and enlightened her grandnephew that she would open his eyes to a world he never dreamt of seeing.

Hektor felt that way about Laura's traveling with him around the globe and called himself "Uncle Mame." Laura still accuses him of having sand in his shoes; Hektor believed he inherited his passion to explore the world from both of his grandfathers. He knew deep in his heart, he was always destined to be a wanderer on the earth.

⚭

Hektor and Laura became vagabonds and sailed the seven seas; there is hardly a major body of water in the world they haven't explored. Voyaging across the world's oceans and seas, sailing the Mediterranean and Caribbean, rounding the capes of South America and the African Continent, circumnavigating New Zealand and Australia, setting foot on Greenland and Iceland, viewing the North Cape and Spitsbergen, Hektor saw himself as the Flying Dutchman.

Of course, he wasn't condemned to an eternal life at sea but seemed to be driven to explore more of this wonderful, whacky world. The major capitals on all continents, Alaska and Hawaii and the remaining forty-eight of the United States, all provinces of Canada, Mexico, the Great Wall of China, the wildlife of Africa, Victoria Falls, the United Kingdom and Ireland, Scandinavia, Machu Picchu, the Amazon, the Galapagos Islands, Iguazu Falls, Torres del Paine, Antarctica, the South Sea Islands, Dubai, Bhutan, India, Morocco, Viet Nam and Ha Long Bay, Angkor Wat in Cambodia, Russia, Siberia, Japan, Bali, Thailand, the wonders of Egypt, Jordan, and Israel, the Suez and Panama canals, and Costa Rica were seen through their eyes. One might ask, what is left for them to experience?

Well into his eighties, Hektor sometimes wonders when and how the Birken Saga will end. It has been an exciting and often turbulent life. With his loving Laura by his side for more than fifty-five years, they experienced many highs and lows—and did so together. They finally realized the years of racing had passed them by; it was time to consider drifting away.

Had he been fortunate enough to still be around, Hektor's good friend Harry would have had the last word in the Birken Saga: *"Douse der Glimmer*; it's been one hell of a ride!"

Harald's Garland
A Collection of Short Stories

Rise and Fall of the Hahnenkamms

"DID you hear that?"

"How could I not. It sounded sort of muffled. You see that pale blue Mercedes ahead? It looks like it's smashed against the side of the house on the corner. Let's approach with caution. I have a strange feeling about this one, Franz."

Adolf jumped out of the car, his hand reaching for the gun in his holster. "Come close, Franz, and give me a good flash into *Pale Blue.*" The light bounced off the smooth leather covering of the dashboard. Adolf gasped. "Franz, we heard right a few seconds ago. Look at the guy in the driver's seat. What's left of him. Half his face is gone. Get on the horn and call for backup. This one's too big to handle just for the two of us. Don't touch a friggin' thing before you put on some gloves!"

Sirens were blaring as they approached the corner of Rosalinden-strasse. People were pouring out of neighboring houses or leaning from windows as three blue-flashing cruisers reached the area near the accident. *An accident*—at least that's what the curious onlookers suspected. All they saw was the pale-blue Mercedes smashed against the corner of Rosalindenstrasse 36. Officers Friedrichs and Meister made sure no one got close enough to glance at the dead man inside the car.

Sergeant Apfelbaum was the first to exit from one of the police cars among those summoned for backup. "What happened here? Why the call for assistance? Looks like a fender bender to me! Are we dealing with a drunken bum who got a bit too close to his own house? What's your name?" He faced officer Friedrichs. "Are you two new on the force?"

"Adolf Friedrichs, Precinct Thirty-seven." He clicked his heels. "My partner is Franz Meister. We've been on the force since 1986. Just patrolling the neighborhood. We were about a block from the scene when both of us heard a muffled, popping sound. We thought it sounded like a gunshot. That's what prompted us to investigate. Spotting the dead man behind the wheel, I instructed Meister to call for backup. We haven't touched a thing. All is exactly the way we found it. Shall we get rid of the onlookers? No doubt we are looking at a crime scene."

"You're damn right; it wasn't just a fender bender," added Meister.

Apfelbaum aimed his bullhorn, blasting his message to the bystanders. "Folks, you better head back to bed. This ain't a movie set. We have no need for extras. Unless you saw or heard anything we should know, don't bother to stick around. So clear out—*schnell, schnell* [quickly]. We've got our work cut out for us."

As his vision swept over the crowd, he saw a guy approaching the vehicle, his camera pointed at the dead driver. "Did you not understand me? Hand me that camera, you damn fool. You are interfering with a police investigation!"

Totally caught off guard, the man turned over his camera to Apfelbaum. With a single deft motion, Apfelbaum flipped open the back of the camera and ripped the film off its spool. He tossed the cellulite snake into the guy's face. "I hope this teaches you a lesson. You are lucky; I'm a Leica buff myself. Had it been any other brand, I would have kicked the shit out of it." He practically shoved the camera into the offender's gut. *"Now beat it!"*

Apfelbaum and his crew peered into the vehicle; the driver's suit coat was oozing with congealing blood. One of the men opened the door of the Mercedes on the driver's side. Apfelbaum got the full picture. *"Holy shit!* He's wearing pigskin gloves and is gripping a Glock 17 with his left hand. Don't touch that gun until we check for prints, Sattler. He must have fired that thing with his left paw. Put your safety gloves on before searching the body and car. Check the glove compartment for registration and insurance documents. We might learn who this guy is—or should I say: *was?*"

Moritz Sattler, Apfelbaum's partner, started the search of the car. He stared at the papers facing him. "The vehicle is registered to a Ferdinand Hahnenkamm." Glancing briefly at the right side of the man's face he volunteered: "He's a mess, but this guy doesn't look like he's 85 years old. Maybe we are looking at stolen wheels?"

Apfelbaum yelled, "Keep searching."

Two of Apfelbaum's young sidekicks dragged the bloody remains out of the Mercedes and placed the corpse into a body bag. Apfelbaum's voice carried over the sirens from the approaching paddy wagon that would carry the dead man away: "Don't leave any stones unturned when you strip him at the morgue. Under the circumstances, a thorough search of anything he wears must be conducted if we are to learn who he is. Sattler, you ride in the paddy. I'll see you at the morgue."

No sooner did the sirens of the departing vehicle fade in the distance, when a tow truck appeared around the corner and hauled *Pale Blue* away. Windows darkened as gawking neighbors retired one by one. For the disappointed onlookers, the late-night show was over. For the men in blue, solving the mystery of the dead man found at Rosalindenstrasse 36 had just begun.

⋊

Sergeant Apfelbaum stormed into the morgue. "What'ya find in his pockets? Anything? And don't give me that shit. *Nothing!* He must have had something in all those damn pockets."

The coroner came to Sattler's defense as he stood next to the naked corpse covered with a clean white sheet. "He helped me strip this guy. He turned every pocket inside out. That's his wallet. There were two hundred and twelve marks and fifty *Pfennigs* in the wallet in the right back pocket of his pants. The only other things we found were a dirty handkerchief soaked in blood in the left breast pocket of his suit jacket and eight chips from the Siegburg Casino in his left front pant pocket. They were coated with his blood and only identifiable after we washed off the sticky mess. We checked the gun for fingerprints. There were none. Wiped clean. The guy carried neither a driver's license nor mandatory personal ID. Sattler could not have been more thorough in his search."

"Whadya think happened, Doc? You got any ideas?" posed Apfelbaum.

"At this point I'm unwilling to call it suicide although one might assume that's the case from the way he gripped that revolver with his left hand. Sure was a direct hit to his artery on the left side of his face. Either he, or whoever shot him, knew what they were doing.

"You know your next step. Find out who Ferdinand Hahnenkamm, the apparent owner of the car, is. That's the best lead you have at the moment. Your buddy, Sattler, was right. It ain't the guy lying on that table. This man is somewhere in his late forties. At worst, in his early fifties. According to the documents in the glove compartment, the guy Ferdinand Hahnenkamm would be eighty-five. *And that age—this one is not!*"

"Let me take another peek at our friend." Apfelbaum pulled back the sheet, exposing most of the corpse. "Is that his natural hair color? Looking at the color of his skin and his body hair, he looks more like a redhead than that dark color on his scalp. I hadn't noticed that in the darkness of the car. The mess of all the blood sure didn't help. You cleaned him up good!" Coroner Diebel faced the sergeant; he cringed at Apfelbaum's language.

"Absolutely. Just look carefully at the center of his scalp. Without a doubt, this deep auburn is not the man's natural hair color. No question, it's a good dye job. Makes you wonder. He did have a pretty good crop of hair before the insult. The touches of grey on his right temple gave me a hint of his age," said Coroner Diebel.

"I'll check on Ferdinand Hahnenkamm first thing in the morning. That Mercedes has been around for a few years, although it looks in great shape on the outside. It's a 190-E Benz. Good car. Of course, after the shooting, it will need major work on the inside and some restoration on the outside where he got too close to the building. For now, it's impounded until this case is solved. I need to get some sleep; I was supposed to be off duty three hours ago," stated Apfelbaum.

Diebel covered up the corpse before he shoved the gurney into the ice box and slammed the steel door with vigor. An autopsy would be done in the morning. "Night, gentlemen! You'll have the full report later tomorrow."

〤

Apfelbaum was at his desk by 9 in the morning. He was nursing his second cup of coffee when he reached for his phone. He dialed the Motor Vehicle Bureau.

"Motor Vehicle Registration, "Fräulein Reif speaking. How may I direct your call?"

"Sergeant Apfelbaum, Precinct #41. We impounded a Mercedes

190-E after a shooting last night. The documents in the car suggest that the vehicle belonged to a Ferdinand Hahnenkamm. I need a little more info on the owner. Can you help me? Or who can?"

"I believe I can check that for you. Was that Hahnenkamm with two 'Ms'?"

"Yes'm!"

"Just a moment, please." Five minutes went by. Apfelbaum was tapping his desk with his pen, a nervous habit of his. He wasn't the most patient man on the force. He heard Fräulein Reif pick up the receiver.

"Ferdinand Hahnenkamm was born in 1910. He bought the car new in 1983. Our records indicate that he died in May 1990. His wife signed the title over to their son, Walter, in August 1990."

"You got any dope on the wife and son?" More tapping on the desk.

"All we have on her is her birth date and the year she died. She's from 1911 and died in 1995. Walter, their son, was born in 1947. He's been involved in several serious car accidents. Hahnenkamm Jr. has been in the clink twice for DUI—big time. His last residence of record is Rosalindenstrasse 36 in Essen. That's all I have for you without further digging!"

"Thanks, Fräulein Reif. That's a heck of a lot more than we had last night." He replaced the phone on his desk — none too gently.

"I'll be damned. Doc Diebel was right on with the estimate of this guy's age. He was 49 in June. Sattler, you got it right too. You were wondering last night if he slammed that car into his house; and that is exactly what he did. Supposedly he lives at the corner house where we found him. Let's hightail it over there and find out what's that all about."

Apfelbaum and Sattler jumped into an unmarked cruiser and were on their way. They pulled up in front of Rosalindenstrasse 36 in no time flat. "Not too much damage to the house," noted Sattler.

They walked up to the house entrance and checked out the names shown by each door bell.

"There's a W. Hahnenkamm shown on the second floor." Apfelbaum pressed the doorbell repeatedly without getting any response. "You think he was a bachelor? Him lying in the morgue would be 'splaining why no one answers the door. Wanna try ringing the neighbor on the same floor? Who knows?" Sattler shrugged his shoulders and looked at the name. "It's a weird one. Dingdong? I'd change that in a heartbeat if I were stuck with that handle." Sattler laid his thumb on the button and pressed firmly. A buzzer sounded and the door opened.

Clutching the highly polished wooden bannister, the two cops climbed the stairs to the second floor. "Nice to see an old house so well taken care of. I noticed on the cornerstone it was built in 1906. Obviously, it must have survived WWII," commented Sattler.

Catching their breath, they were greeted by Lady Dingdong, clearly advanced in age. She was puzzled to see the two uniformed men standing in front of her. They flashed their police badges and introduced themselves properly. Apfelbaum spoke first.

"Sergeant Apfelbaum!" As he stuck out his right hand to greet the woman. "This is my colleague, Sergeant Sattler. We are here to investigate an incident that occurred in front of this house after 23:00 last night."

"It gives me pleasure to meet you, officers. I'm Amalia Dingdong. How may I be of service to you? Please step into my parlor. I would like to sit before we proceed. I am eighty-five years old. Although I'm pretty spry for my age, I just don't want to stand here in the hallway and look up at you tall, handsome men during a lengthy conversation. It simply is too hard on my aging neck. Forgive me, what did you say this is about?" The lady extended her hand, inviting Apfelbaum and Sattler into her living room. They glanced around, noticing that it was elegantly furnished. The lady obviously had money and good taste.

"Didn't you hear all the sirens last night? The whole neighborhood seemed to be looking on when we arrived on the scene," said Apfelbaum.

"No. My bedroom is in the back of the house, and when I shed my hearing aids before I retire, I'm pretty much dead to the world. I went to bed shortly after 22:00. I'm the oldest resident in the building. Most of my neighbors work and are gone during the day. I believe, the young Mrs. Hahnenkamm, across from my apartment, is on vacation. She and her twelve-year-old son have been gone for a few weeks. I heard her tell another neighbor, they planned to visit her relatives outside of Stuttgart. She and her husband, Walter, own this house. I rarely see him; he seems to be shining in absence."

As she spoke, Apfelbaum and Sattler were watching Lady Dingdong closely. They winked at each other, both registering that apparently she didn't share particular fondness for her neighbors, the Hahnenkamms.

"Would you care for tea or coffee? I have both. If it was later in the day, I might have offered you a cognac. Of course, I realize, this is not a social call and you are not to imbibe while you are on duty."

"Right Ma'am. No cognac for sure, but I wouldn't mind a cup of coffee. What about you, Sattler?"

"Sounds great. It's been a short night. I'll take mine with a healthy dash of cow. No sugar, please."

"No cow for me, but three lumps of sugar would do the trick."

It took no time at all for Frau Dingdong to reappear. "Here we are, gentlemen." She set the pretty collectors' cups in front of them.

"Do you by any chance know of a way we could get a hold of Frau Hahnenkamm? It's pretty important we do. We found her husband shot to death in front of this house last night. He was seated in a pale blue Mercedes; he apparently rammed into the side of this building before he died. He's in the precinct morgue; an autopsy is being performed as we speak."

"Oh, my God!" Was all she said loudly. She turned her face away from the police officers. In an almost unvoiced aside she muttered: "Good riddance to the bastard!"

"What were you saying, Ma'am?" said Apfelbaum.

"Oh, I was just sending a quiet, short message to the Man upstairs. That's too bad. I'm glad his mother didn't live to experience this. She's been gone for a little over a year. She was my closest friend from the time we were little girls. We were born the same year, attended the same schools, and treasured the good and the bad years we were destined to share. I miss Elsa terribly. Such a kind lady. She outlived Ferdinand by five years.

"I'm sorry to say, I have no clue where the young woman's family lives. I know it's in the vicinity of Stuttgart. I never had an amicable relationship with the young folks, although I've known Walter since the day he was born. How well I remember."

"Pray, tell. Would you mind telling us a bit about young Hahnenkamm now lying dead in our morgue?"

"Not at all. He was an unexpected godsend to my dear friend!"

"Where do I begin? I suppose at the beginning. Elsa and I were born a week apart not too far from this house; that is, I was born a couple of streets over from Rosalindenstrasse. Elsa was actually born in this very house. At the time, the building was merely five years old. It was her father's pride and joy. Elsa's mother often told the story of the *Richtfest* [the day when a young tree was mounted on the almost completed roof, symbolizing the establishment of the house's roots with the promise of a long and prosperous life]. Elsa and I met the day we started in Kindergarten. My God, that was eighty years ago. Where have the years gone? We were four years old when our fathers marched off to fight for Germany in the "Great War.""

"That's a long time ago. Are you sure you are up to sharing the whole story of the Hahnenkamms' lives with us?" said Apfelbaum.

"I won't go into all parcels of the Hahnenkamms' lives; they only came into play in 1932 when Elsa married Ferdinand. She was such a beautiful bride. My story begins with the life of my dear friend, Elsa Krämer.

"She had an older sister and brother at the time. Her younger sister was born when Elsa was eight years old. Georgine was our living doll until we outgrew playing with dolls. By the time we were in our teens, Georgine was a handful. Her father spoiled the heck out of her. Georgine never could do any wrong."

"Well, are we ever getting to the present, dear lady? How much time you believe we have?" interrupted Sergeant Apfelbaum.

"My good man, if you want me to take you into the present, you'll have to suffer with me through the past. That's all there is to that. Would you two care for another cup of coffee? At the rate we are going, we may sample my Remy Martin or LOUIS XIII after all."

"Heh, nothing but the best, lady! For now, let's stick with the coffee. May I use your phone. I better let my superior know that we are onto something and that we may be gone for a while."

He dialed the number at Precinct #41. "Apfelbaum here; put me through to Kirsch."

"Commander Kirsch speaking."

"Hi. It's Apfelbaum. We made some interesting discoveries at the Hahnenkamm house. The guy's wife is out of town, and no one knows where she and their kid are visiting. Closest I got, they are somewhere near Stuttgart. That covers a lot of territory. Their next door neighbor, a delightful 85-year-old lady, is filling us in on some interesting background." He winked at Amalia Dingdong.

"The lady isn't too friendly toward the young Mrs. Hahnenkamm, the guy in the morgue, and their 12-year-old son. On the other hand, she is a gold mine of info re the older Hahnenkamms. We may be a while. Some of what she has to say might shed light on the case. Hope you don't mind. Sattler and I are sitting at the edge of our seats. See you sometime. Not sure when."

"You do as you see fit. Sounds like we are going to have a lengthy visitor in our morgue. Kirsch hung up the phone. Apfelbaum gave Amalia another wink, encouraging her to continue her story. "Thanks for the refill on the coffee." Sattler nodded his head in agreement.

"Elsa Hahnenkamm and I had a wonderful life for most of our years. As we became ancient, so to speak, not all that was gold glittered, especially what concerned Elsa. She should have been Queen for the Day to her last breath. That's why I'm so bitter. But let me take you back to happier days.

"Elsa was always a beautiful girl. She was elegant, well groomed, and stylish in the latest of fashion. I had a hard time keeping up with her. By the time we were 16, we were accomplished dancers. The rake who taught us the latest dances in vogue was Elsa's brother, Arthur. His idol was Fred Astaire.

"We'd walk into the Kasanova on his arms all decked out in the latest flapper dresses and he always in black tie and tux. It never failed, when our threesome showed up, we'd stop the show. The band would switch to a quickstep or the latest tango or foxtrot, and Arthur would present one of us on the *parquet* to the full applause of those in the house. When Arthur and we walked in, other dancers cleared the floor. At first they called Arthur and Elsa "Fred and Adele;" later it was "Fred & Ginger." Everyone adored them.

"I don't remember how often Elsa was the Queen of the Rose Monday parade during Carnival. Twice, I was her first attendant. We truly enjoyed our lives. Arthur had taught Elsa to drive; by 1929 she had her own car. Tooting around Essen in Elsa's sporty little number, the two of us were viewed as being notorious by other jealous females.

"Neither Elsa nor I were particularly interested in pursuing academics. She got into the habit of working a few hours in the parental business and I enjoyed finishing school being groomed for that "MRS" degree. Our free time was dedicated to Arthur's motto *"live, live, live!"* His father wanted him to be a lawyer or physician. He chose to be a butcher in the daytime and a dancer and bar fly at night. Arthur practiced what he preached. He *lived!*

"All that carousing came to a screeching halt when Elsa and I were married to a couple of great guys in 1932. As a matter of fact, we were married the same day in the same church. It was almost like a double wedding. Elsa was a stunning bride on the arm of her ailing father being led into the arms of Ferdinand Hahnenkamm, a well-to-do gent from Wanne-Eickel—of all places. I married Otto Dingdong.

"I almost insisted on keeping my maiden name, Amalia Dorothea von Eichendorff. I'm a great-great-great-great, etc., daughter of Joseph Freiherr von Eichendorff, a famous 19th century Prussian poet, novelist, playwright, literary critic, translator, and anthologist. It took a mad love for my future husband not to object to becoming a Dingdong. I was always glad there were no little Dingdongs to worry about. Even after Otto was killed in Stalingrad, the thought never occurred to me to change back to my maiden name. I know it's the source of much amusement for most people—including you two gentlemen. I couldn't help reading the smirks on your faces when first I introduced myself to you. That's OK. I've gotten used to it in sixty-four years."

"Sorry, we were so obvious. It's not your name that is important to us; it's your charm and the delightful telling and sharing of the Hahnenkamms' story you're willing to impart to us that captivates and keeps us listening to you," said Apfelbaum. Sattler smiled in agreement.

"At first, Elsa and I suffered from separation anxiety when she and Ferdinand settled in Wanne-Eickel where his ancestral home and business were located. Of course, we realized quickly that we weren't worlds apart and could easily visit each other by hopping on a train and be there in less than an hour.

"Otto was a rising star in the banking world, and Ferdinand was successful in expanding the familial enterprise. Both Elsa and I enjoyed a certain degree of affluence, affording us the elegant homes in which we lived. Arthur married a couple years later and took over his father's business in Essen. Clearly, those fun-filled days of the roaring twenties were behind us.

"Somehow the turbulent changes on the political horizon didn't impact any of us as much as they did many others until all suitable young men were drawn into WWII in 1939. What Elsa and I regretted the most in the early years of our respective marriages was the fact that we were not meant to have children. Elsa was fortunate enough to have two nephews by her older sister, Helena. Being godmother to both boys filled a certain void in her life. Being an only child, I was denied that experience.

"After Ferdinand was inducted, Elsa closed their business in Wanne-Eickel and spent much time traveling and with her family in Essen. She and I were closer than ever, especially when I was widowed in 1942 and Arthur went MIA during the military debacle called Stalingrad.

"While my home in Rüttenscheid survived the war unscathed, Elsa's home in Wanne-Eickel was flattened during a bombing in 1944; the parental home on Rosalindenstrasse was severely damaged in 1945. Elsa had no idea what happened to Ferdinand during the waning months of the war. I was fortunate enough to have Elsa share my home during the twilight of the Third Reich and the collapse of the country. Both of us were stunned when Ferdinand appeared at our doorstep looking more like an escapee from a concentration camp than the healthy-looking young man both of us recalled. He showed up in August 1945.

Sattler coughed, getting Amalia's attention. "Ma'am, after all this coffee, I need to use a restroom. Could you point me in the right direction?"

"Oh, of course. Down that hall; it's the second door on your left.

Both of you, feel free to use it. I should have thought of that myself." When Sattler returned, Apfelbaum excused himself to do the same. Amalia went to her bedroom, needing a potty break herself.

"What do you think, Sattler? This is turning into quite the story. I can't wait for her to get to the juicy stuff. I know we are still officially on duty. Hope you don't mind, but the next time she offers me some of that fancy cognac of hers, I won't decline. I'm even considering accepting a bite to eat if she should ask."

"I thought you would never come up with that suggestion. I've been ready for a shot and some munchies for the last hour or so."

"Glad to know you're seeing it my way. Here she comes. Let's see if she reads our minds," said Apfelbaum.

"Thanks for letting me take a little break. I needed that. Now, how about a little refreshment? I have the fixings for some *Schnittchen* [finger sandwiches] in the house. What may I serve you to drink, gentlemen? Would you care for some cognac or something different?"

"We thought you'd never ask. No, just joking," said Armstrong. "I'll relieve you of some of that fancy LOUIS XIII. What about you, Sattler? I know cognac is not exactly your speed."

"If you have it, I'll have a Dortmunder and a shot of *Schnapps,* anything but cognac. Thanks."

"No problem. It's all on hand; I'm delighted with your company. At my age, most of my friends are gone. Not having family or friends, it becomes a lonely existence. It's not often that I get to entertain two handsome young officers. Never mind "entertain." It seems I have you enthralled listening to the telling of my story." She got up and reached for a crystal snifter, pouring a healthy drink for Armstrong. "I'll be right back with your *Bier* and a shot." After both men had their drinks, she excused herself for a few moments, wanting to fix the finger sandwiches in her very modern kitchen.

"May we help you with that, Ma'am," inquired Sattler. "No need for that. You men enjoy your drinks, relax, and rest your ears. I won't be long. Haven't done this in a long while. Always loved to entertain. It's my distinct pleasure to have you in my home."

Fifteen minutes later she walked in with a large platter of enticingly arranged finger sandwiches. They might have been prepared by a top-notch deli in the neighborhood. She placed napkins and China plates on the cocktail table and encouraged them to help themselves. "How about refreshing your drinks before I join you for a bite?"

"Thanks, that would be nice. What are you drinking?" said Apfelbaum.

"Nothing alcoholic. I'll have some Perrier. I need to keep my wits about me if you want me to finish my tale of the Hahnenkamms.

"As I said, before we decided to take a break, Elsa and I were both stunned by Ferdinand's reappearance. At the time, I was the first to find my voice: 'Where have you been? How did you find Elsa and me?'

"'When I found myself on the doorstep of Helena's house, I scared the hell out of all of them. They thought they were seeing a ghost. It was from Helena that I learned of your existence. And that's how I got here and found you.'

⋈

"'East of Vienna, I became separated from my company during the last skirmishes and engagements with Russian troops. When the artillery fire ceased, I crawled out of the woods and hid in a farmer's barn for two days. I took off my uniform and put it under some hay in the barn. All I had on was my dirty underwear and sox and boots. I must have been quite a sight when I finally emerged from my hiding place and faced the old farmer and his wife. They were scared shitless, believing at first I was a Russian deserter. When I addressed them in German, they were relieved and offered me shelter for a couple of days. I was thankful to them for feeding me.

"'The old man was kind enough to part with the best of his old pre-war bicycles. I started on the first leg of my long journey home to Wanne-Eickel as dusk set in. For the first two hundred miles, I moved from town to town and from barn to barn mostly at dusk and in early evening. Some farmers never even realized that I had slept in their barn for a few hours. Here and there, I became daring enough and faced an owner and begged for a piece of bread or whatever. Most nights I devoured half-ripened apples I had ripped off trees as I was riding by on my bike. When the bike gave out, I hoofed it. It took me more than three months to conquer the one thousand kilometers plus to reach home.'"

"Man, that was some hike when you stop and think about it," interrupted Apfelbaum. "You ain't kidding," agreed Sattler.

Amalia smiled as she continued her tale: "Ferdinand made a remarkable recovery; within a few weeks, he returned to Wanne-Eickel and began to build a humble structure on the site of their former business and home. None of their personal belongings were destroyed due to Elsa's foresight to transport anything of value to safe storage with relatives living in Swabia in 1943.

"When Arthur did not return by late 1946, Elsa's parents encouraged Ferdinand to assume responsibility for their business in Rüttenscheid. Elsa and I were elated that she would remain close to me in Essen.

"Within weeks, a joyous Elsa hugged me on my doorstep. 'You'll never believe this. I'm with child and will be a mother by next June. Can you imagine this after being married to Ferdinand for more than fourteen years? He is positively euphoric.'

"So was I. Getting over my first shock after learning of Elsa's good fortune, I was jealous and envious of her. How I would have loved to have a child by my dear Otto— Dingdong or not. It wasn't meant to be, I consoled myself and looked forward to the birth of Elsa's child."

⋊⋉

"Walter Hahnenkamm was born as anticipated in late June 1947. Elsa didn't really suffer a difficult birth. When the baby slipped from her womb and announced its arrival with a healthy outburst of energy, Elsa was overjoyed to learn that she had delivered a boy who would carry on the family name. The baby was rushed from the birthing room; he was washed and dressed before being presented to his parents.

"By the time the nurse brought little Walter to Elsa's room for a first viewing, Ferdinand was standing next to her bed anxious to behold their creation. They placed the baby into her arms and she counted his cute little fingers; the toes had to wait until later. Gently, she removed the tiny knit hat from his scalp. Elsa couldn't believe her eyes. She screamed: '*Oh my God*, he has a head full of carrot-red hair!'

"She sobbed uncontrollably as she looked up at Ferdinand."

"'You have dark hair, and I'm a blonde; how did we wind up with a red-haired kid?'

"One would have thought she had given birth to a monster. Ferdinand finally spoke."

"'Remember, both my father and my older brother, Junker, have red hair. It's in the family for sure. The milkman had nothing to do with it!'

"Once she recovered from the initial shock, she voiced her solution to the 'problem' as she saw it."

"'Hydrogen peroxide does wonders for my hair; why not for him?'

"Within days of being discharged from the hospital and much to the shock of everyone in the family, little Walter was transformed into a bleached blonde. He remained a blonde until six months before he started Kindergarten. Elsa reluctantly appeased Ferdinand and let Walter be a natural redhead. By this time, the carrot red had darkened to a somewhat more acceptable shade as far as Elsa saw it.

There was no question about it, Walter was terribly indulged by both of his parents but also very much loved. They had never expected to celebrate parenthood.

"Walter was given every opportunity to succeed in whatever whimsy he elected to pursue, be it his attempt at being a musician, an ice skater, a race car driver, or whatever. He even tried his hand at becoming a butcher. He never truly became accomplished at anything; the closest he came was to being somewhat gifted at being a hockey player. And, of course, he became extremely skilled at spending his parent's money.

"By the time he was eighteen, he had smashed three new Mercedes, including the one he had received as a present from his father. In his mid-twenties, he had actually become a rather handsome male. His hair was always professionally styled and dyed a dark auburn.

"To his parents' chagrin, he announced that he was marrying a girl of whom they knew little. The girl's parents were poor, and Walter expected Elsa and Ferdinand to pay for an elaborate wedding. The girl was pregnant with his child.

"I was invited to the wedding celebration. After dinner, Elsa and I needed to use the ladies' room. While using the facility, the bride and her attendants walked in and proceeded to discuss vociferously how successful they had been in duping the groom and his family into believing that the bride was knocked up. Their plan was to milk the Hahnenkamms for all they were worth.

"Needless to say, they were flabbergasted when Elsa and I emerged from our respective stalls. The bride had not envisioned meeting the wrath of God in the ladies' room when Elsa turned on her: 'You cheap piece of trash. You and your entire tribe better be out of the establishment within fifteen minutes. Take a good look at our son as you pass him by. It's the last time you will see him other than in court when your marriage will be annulled. You'll never see another mark from this family!'

"Elsa then walked up to Ferdinand and told him what she had discovered. 'Tell our son, the party is over!!'

"She picked up her purse and settled the bill with the restaurateur in cash. Walter had never seen his mother so angry and in such a state. Once again though, his parents shielded him from assuming his responsibilities. Of course, in this case they protected him as well as themselves."

"Mrs. Dingdong, this is beginning to sound more revealing by the minute. Our man in the morgue is indeed a person of interest. Sattler and I can't wait to hear the end of this story."

"Walter married a second time when he was thirty-six and presented his parents with a grandson the following year. Horst was seen as the joy in Elsa and Ferdinand's autumn years. They had moved into an elegant modern apartment in the neighborhood that particularly suited Elsa. The responsibilities of managing the large house and business were turned over to their son. Grandson Horst was going on six years when Ferdinand suffered a massive heart attack. He knew he hadn't long to live when he spoke to Elsa.

"'Watch out for our son. He's a bad seed. Never divest yourself of anything, and never sign anything without benefit of legal counsel. I've done everything in my power to protect you. There are things you do not know about our son, matters which I've settled not wanting to upset you. Elsa, mark my words, and never forget what I'm trying to tell you. I hope he doesn't end like my brother, Junker, who gambled away his fortune. They found him in an alley in Witten; he had shot himself in a drunken stupor.'

"Ferdinand fell back into Elsa's arms. He was dead.

"Less than two years had passed when Walter made his first move."

"'Mother, if you want us to continue living in the old house, you must spend *beaucoups* money and update that mausoleum. I need at least one hundred thousand marks to make that place livable for us.

We deserve to live in the style to which we've become accustomed. Don't give me any crap; I'm well aware of how much money you have in your bank accounts. I could ask you for my share of the inheritance, which is fifty percent of what Father left you. But I won't; I'm not that stupid. I want it all by the time I'm done with you. And you better meet my demands if you want to see Horst again.'

"He slammed her purse on the table."

"'Write the fucking check before I beat the shit out of you!'

"Elsa wrote the check for one hundred thousand marks and handed it to her son. As soon as he left the apartment, she called me and told me what happened. When I arrived at her place, she was sobbing and practically fainted in my arms. I always had some inkling of what might happen after Ferdinand's death. But never had I dreamt of witnessing such depravity. This was just the opening salvo.

"By the time Horst was eight years old, he was told by his father to kick the old lady in the shins if she didn't fork over what he demanded. Walter insisted that he be the sole agent to collect all rents from properties owned by Elsa. When she refused to sign the documents, he had her declared mentally incompetent by a physician, only too willing to accept the *thirty pieces of silver* for the ugly deed. After Elsa's eighty-first birthday, he moved his mother out of her elegant apartment with most of her furnishings into the oldest and smallest apartment in this old house. It was the only part of the building never updated since 1906. With furniture piled to the ceilings, the tiny hovel resembled an ugly warehouse. Anything suitable for a quick sale was turned into cash.

"Walter and his wife Elke lived in the thoroughly modern quarters above her and provided Elsa with minimal and substandard nourishment, had her telephone service cut, and controlled who she might see. And that included me; her captors didn't want me to look after her. I had to sneak downstairs in the dark when I wanted to see Elsa.

"The name of the previous tenants of the tiny apartment was 'Nix'. Elke insisted on not changing the name tag at the house directory. In her opinion, the name suited her mother-in-law. [*Nix*, in German slang, means *nothing*.] Elsa's heirs thought of her and treated her indeed as if she was *nothing*. They had every intent of starving her to death. After she had a mild stroke, she was hospitalized in quarters meeting the needs of the poorest of the poor. Upon being discharged, Walter and Elke transferred Elsa to a home for the indigent. It was there that she died in 1995. She was buried next to Ferdinand in the family plot without adding her name on the grave marker. Walter made sure his mother remained *"Nix"* even in death. At last, he had made good on his word; Walter had taken his mother for all she had—her dignity, her wealth, and ultimately—her life."

"That brings us to the present," said officer Apfelbaum. "I suppose we could get a warrant and search their apartment in his wife's absence. I would like to have a photo of Walter before we take a ride out to the Casino in Siegburg. That should be our next step. You don't by any chance have a fairly recent photo of the gentleman, do you?"

"Don't call him a gentleman in my presence. He was a monster. Now I can share with you my softly spoken aside when we first met this morning. I said: 'Good riddance to the bastard'— and I meant it. To answer your question, I have a photo of him and Ferdinand that was taken about six years ago shortly before his father died. He hasn't changed all that much, especially with that professionally styled hair and dye job. Anyone who knew him well enough would recognize him. Let me get it for you; it's in one of my drawers in the desk in my bedroom. I couldn't keep it on display after what that scumbag did to my friend." Amalia left Apfelbaum and Sattler alone for a moment.

"Let's stop at the office and pick up those chips before heading for Siegburg. We'll briefly fill in Kirsch if he's still on duty. I want the goods on this guy," said Apfelbaum. Sattler had had other plans for the evening but concurred with his colleague that a night visit might be a better time to get info re the habits of a certain Walter Hahnenkamm.

When Amalia returned with the photo in question, Apfelbaum clued her in on their intent to pay a visit to the Siegburg Casino that very night.

"Here are our business cards. Please get in touch with us as soon as Frau Hahnenkamm should appear. We've decided not to make any effort to search for her and will keep this out of the papers for as long as possible. Only when we know more about this character shall we proceed. In the meantime, stay in touch with us as soon as you see the whites of Elke Hahnenkamm's eyes—and let's not forget "darling" little Horst. It's been a pleasure being with you Amalia Dorothea von Eichendorff Dingdong."

"The pleasure has been all mine, officers." She shook their hands and smiled broadly as Apfelbaum and Sattler departed.

)X(

"Hit the gas pedal, Sattler. I was glad they hadn't locked up Hahnenkamm's stuff in the evidence locker. It was sort of surprising but fortunate for us. I bet you Kirsch wasn't aware of the slip. Diebel must have been bushed after that late-night arrival. Had Kirsch seen that, the shit would've hit the fan!"

)X(

They walked into the Siegburg Casino an hour later and headed straight for one of the busiest roulette tables. Apfelbaum sidled up to the croupier and paid close attention to what the man was doing. Looking at the chips on the table, he knew that the ones recovered from Hahnenkamm's pant pockets had indeed originated at the Siegburg Casino.

A number of players lost considerable amounts of money and walked away from the table. There was a momentary lull in activities when Apfelbaum seized the opportunity. He held up Walter's photograph to the croupier. He could tell immediately that Walter was no stranger to the man.

"Do you know this gentleman?" With that, both he and Sattler flashed their credentials. "May we go someplace where we can talk? It's urgent business. What's your name?"

"Herrmann Meier. Let me get my boss's attention." He raised his arm, waving it repeatedly.

Finally, a well-dressed gent approached. "What's this about? Is there a problem? I'm Fritz Deerendorf, the Casino manager."

Apfelbaum responded.

"Nice meeting you. There's no problem; we just have a question or two about an apparent frequent patron of your Casino. Do you recognize this man? Obviously, Meier did when he glanced at the photo a moment ago."

"Let me see it. *Oh, yes*! We know Herr Hahnenkamm very well. He spends many hours indeed at our gaming tables. Lately, he hasn't been too lucky. As a matter of fact, yesterday he lost his shirt at that table over there!"

"May we talk in your offices for a moment? We'd rather not entertain your patrons and stop Meier, here, from making more money for the house."

"OK, you are catching us on a slow night. Step right in, gentlemen, and have a seat. Now, what can I do for you?"

"When you said Hahnenkamm lost his shirt, how elegant a shirt was it?"

"He lost eighty-five thousand marks just last night. That was about the worst day he had this week. Actually, he wrote us an IOU for twenty thousand. Is there a problem?"

"Did you see him leave? Was he sober, or did he have too much to drink?"

"Don't tell me he was in an accident? Actually, I thought he was pretty sober when he got into that old *Pale Blue* that used to be his dad's."

"Did he have any words with anyone here before he gave you the IOU and left?"

"No. He certainly had no words with me. I knew he'd be good for his debts; he's never stiffed us out of anything."

"I must tell you, Herr Deerendorf," Apfelbaum cleared his throat, stalling to get the man's full attention, "Walter Hahnen-kamm is dead. He drove *Pale Blue* home and got a bit too close to the side of his own house. When he was found by a couple of our men on routine night patrol, he was seated inside the car. The left side of his face was blown away by a point-blank shot to his head. He was dead when they found him. Can you think of anyone who might have done him in? Also, do you recall if he was a lefty?"

"I can't believe what you are telling me. How is that possible? Yes, he was quite the gambler, but he was very much liked by all patrons and our staff. He was Mr. Debonair. He always came alone to the Casino. Once he ran into one of our regulars, a lady — Madame Georgine. They didn't speak to one another. He told me later she was his mother's younger sister and that they were arch enemies. He never drank much. Perhaps a cocktail, a beer, or a glass of wine. I've never seen him drunk and never act as anything but a gentleman."

Apfelbaum swallowed hard as he mouthed to Sattler: "Must be a case of dual personality."

"Heh, I almost forgot. He was a lefty. Saw him write, eat, smoke, etc.— always with his left hand," said Deerendorf.

"Thanks for your cooperation and the info on Hahnenkamm. We have a much better picture, Herr Deerendorf. We'll see ourselves out. Thanks again."

They put on their caps and walked out to the car. Meier looked busy when they walked by his roulette table.

"What's your verdict, Sattler? Was it murder or suicide? Any intuition about it?"

"Knowing what we know now, and Hahnenkamm apparently very skilled in using his left hand, I'm inclined to believe he did it himself. We need to do a little checking into his finances. That will be another important clue."

"I concur. Exactly my feeling. We'll do some checking tomorrow. Let's call it a day after dropping off Hahnenkamm's stuff at the lock box. We'll fill in Kirsch and write the report tomorrow morning. I'm bushed. It's been one hell of a day and night!"

Sattler, jokingly clicked his heels. "My sentiments, exactly!" said he as he walked toward his motorbike.

Apfelbaum spotted the night secretary. "Are you by any chance super busy? If not, would you be so good and transcribe my tape for the chief? Just put it on his desk when you are done. Very interesting! Very interesting, indeed! Thanks!"

"No problem! Anything for you, Officer Apfelbaum, any time."

)X(

Apfelbaum and Sattler sat across from each other at their double desks. Fräulein Reif had done some digging for them. Both guys picked up their phones on the first ring. Apfelbaum covered his mouthpiece for a split second. "This ought to be good!"

"Yes Fräulein Reif, what'ya find out."

"Sorry, Apfelbaum; it's commander Kirsch. Enlightening report you left on my desk. When on earth did you have the time to write in that much detail? This guy's more colorful than I expected. Guess you can't judge a book by its cover, to use a cliché."

"Actually, we used our noodle for a change. I had my recorder running all the time Amalia Dingdong was talking. We had the night secretary type it up; luckily, it was a slow night."

"Smart move. I see a call coming in. This might be Reif for you. Let me know what she found out."

"Yes, Fräulein Reif. Apfelbaum speaking. Got some juicy details for me?"

"I'm not sure about juicy. I had to reach out to the City Clerk for some of the info. Obviously, I have no access to his bank accounts. By the way, they are all exclusively in his name. Both properties in Wanne-Eickel and in Essen are mortgaged to the max. When he inherited them a year ago, they were debt free. That should tell you something. We might and we might not get access to bank records when Frau Hahnenkamm returns from wherever. It might take a court order should it be deemed necessary to have a look at them."

"Thanks! Very helpful info." He replaced the phone in it's cradle. "Let's have a chat with Kirsch and Diebel. I want to hear what they speculate."

Kirsch closed his office door. "Well, gentlemen, what do you say." Diebel spoke first. "From what I read and have seen and heard, he had good reason to kill himself. What still puzzles me are the use of the gloves and the gun wiped clean of any fingerprints. Why would someone in that state of mind be concerned about leaving fingerprints? I have no problem with him being a lefty. Those who function in that mode become very adept at doing anything effectively."

"Sattler and I wondered the same after initial discussions and findings. After listening for hours to Amalia Dingdong, we figured that bastard was mean enough to make it look like someone murdered him. We share Dr. Diebel's assessment that he committed suicide after that last horrendous loss at the Siegburg Casino. For now, let's keep him on ice until Madame Hahnenkamm returns. That ought to be a shocker for her and that miserable kid of theirs. Amalia Dingdong will call us the moment she hears any signs of life across the hallway. She will not speak to the young woman. It will be up to us to break the news."

)(

Ten days went by before Amalia heard activities across the way. Actually it was Horst maneuvering the stairs on roller skates that alerted her to their presence. She confirmed what she suspected by viewing the annoying activity through her "spy." Horst wasn't aware that he was being observed. It was ten in the morning when she dialed Apfelbaum's extension.

"Hallo, Officer Apfelbaum." He recognized her distinct voice immediately. "Guten Morgen, Frau Dingdong. Any news from across the hallway?"

"Yes! They must have returned late last night. I wonder how she reacted to the empty apartment? I'm sure the bed was untouched, and I doubt he left any kind of note. He never struck me as that considerate. Of course, if he planned his demise before he left that day for another round at the casino, perhaps there was a note. Although, seeing the boy on roller skates in the stairway would indicate to me that Frau Hahnenkamm doesn't have a clue—and I intend to keep it that way. It's all in your hands."

"Thank you, Frau Dingdong. Sattler and I are on our way. We'll be knocking on Frau Hahnenkamm's door shortly. Thanks again for your discretion."

Apfelbaum and Sattler rang the doorbell ten minutes later. They looked at each other walking up to the second floor. There was no doubt in their minds that Frau Dingdong's spy was in use. Elke opened the door and gasped when she saw both men in their blues. "Are you sure you pushed the correct button?" was her greeting.

"Are you Frau Walter Hahnenkamm? If so, you are the person we wish to speak to. Please put on a coat or jacket and come with us."

"Why? And where to? What about my son? He's playing on the street."

"Bring him along. It concerns his father, your husband. We need you at the police station."

Elke's eyes were wide open; she stared at the two officers. She didn't ask another question. On the street, she called Horst over. "Take those skates off and get in this car. We have to go with these men. It's something about your father. Just keep your foul mouth shut." For once, he minded his mother.

✕

Commander Kirsch and the coroner, Dr. Diebel, had staged the morgue scene. The gurney bearing Walter Hahnenkamm had been removed from storage and turned in such a way that any onlookers were first exposed to his relatively unblemished right side. His body was still completely covered with a stark-white sheet.

Apfelbaum and his entourage entered the morgue. Elke wasn't quite certain where this was headed. Somehow she recalled having observed a similar scene in a movie. She was looking back and forth from the men behind the gurney to Apfelbaum and Sattler.

Dr. Diebel couldn't stand the suspense any longer; he wanted to see the reaction on the face of the presumed wife of the dead man in his custody. With a swift motion of his left arm, he pulled back the sheet exposing the right side of Walter's face. Elke screamed as she reached out to her dead husband.

"We are sorry, but we needed you to confirm that this is indeed your husband. He was found dead in his car twelve days ago. We believe he died as the result of a self-inflicted gunshot wound. No one knew where you were; it's for that reason the police couldn't reach you."

"What makes you think he killed himself? Wouldn't he have left me some kind of note? How did you even know who he was and where he lived?"

"All that was possible by linking the car registration and insurance papers for the Mercedes to your husband. The casino chips in his pant pockets led us to Siegburg where your husband lost eighty-five thousand marks early in the evening before he shot himself. There is an IOU for another twenty thousand marks held by the casino. Your house in Wanne-Eickel as well as your house on Rosalindenstrasse no longer belong to you. They are mortgaged to the hilt. We have no idea if there is any money left in your bank accounts. Does this answer your questions?"

"I'm shocked! Please drive us home." She didn't shed a tear; Elke grabbed Horst by the hand as she turned away from her dead husband. Had she seen him from his left side, she would have fainted—all present were certain of that.

"Your husband's car will be released to you later today. Please let us know where you wish it to be towed. The vehicle is in need of some repair and a major detailing job on the inside. The seats in front may need to be replaced. His body will be transferred to the Parkfriedhof by Heidenkamp Funeral Services. Under the circumstances, we believe you would not want an open casket. Correct?"

"Absolutely not!" was all she said.

"Heidenkamp will discuss all details with you. Again, accept our deepest sympathies."

The funeral took place four days later. There was no obituary in the papers. A small paragraph on page three of the *Westdeutsche Allgemeine Zeitung* [WAZ paper] mentioned the accident and the death of forty-nine-year-old Walter Hahnenkamm whose services would be at the Parkfriedhof. Further details were available through Heidenkamp Funeral Services; their telephone number was listed.

Amalia Dingdong read the blip in the WAZ and decided to attend the funeral. She would be disguised by a veil of darkness and remain in the background. While she detested the dead man, he was the son of her closest friend, and she knew him since the day he was born. She suspected a relatively small group of mourners would be in attendance. For that reason alone, Amalia was pleased with herself that she had resolved to take a cab to the Parkfriedhof and pay her respects. Riding in the cab, she thought about Otto, Elsa, and Ferdinand. They were all resting now in close proximity at the cemetery. Otto probably would have chided her for attending "that monster's" funeral and would have called her a hypocrite. *"So what?"* she thought.

When she got to the gravesite, she stood back but still had a good view of the happenings. The service was brief, with no long-winded speeches by the young minister. What happened next, she couldn't believe. She knew she needed to share her observations with officers Apfelbaum and Sattler.

Unobserved, she walked away from the gravesite. She engaged a cabbie and asked to be taken to Precinct #41. When she entered the station, no one was more pleased to see her than her two handsome men in blue. She might have been eighty-five, dressed in stark black, and heavily veiled, but she had a regal bearing and an aura of unmistakable elegance. Amalia Dorothea von Eichendorff Dingdong was a class act.

Apfelbaum and Sattler rose from their chairs immediately extending their right hands in greeting, gently shaking Amalia's gloved hand. "To what do we owe this honor? You are brightening our dreary day with your surprise visit."

"I've just attended Walter Hahnenkamm's funeral at the Parkfriedhof. His wife didn't even see me standing in the background. Aside from that, I was well disguised—don't you agree?"

"Great veil!" said Sattler.

"There were few mourners beside the son, Horst, and his

mother. I believe I counted fourteen other people. None I knew, and none who knew me. The minister conducted the service with extreme efficiency. They barely started tossing the first shovel of dirt on the coffin when a stunning black Mercedes limousine pulled up right in front of the gravesite. The chauffeur jumped from his seat, opening the left rear door. An elegantly attired blonde stepped out and carried a large bouquet of expensive red roses in her arms. You should have seen *her* black dress and hat. *And those legs*. You men would have gone gaga. She stepped right in front of Elke, the wife, and tossed the roses into the grave. As she did, she turned to face Elke Hahnenkamm. I couldn't help hearing what she said: *'I'm also Frau Walter Hahnenkamm. He built a beautiful home for me and our daughter in Mühlheim. You will hear from my attorney in short order.'* She quickly rushed back to her car. The chauffeur held the backdoor open for her and hurriedly pulled away from the scene. All, including myself, were left speechless."

"I'll be damned! A bigamist to boot!" was all Apfelbaum could say as he struck his desk with his right fist. Sattler suffered momentary *Maulsperre* [lockjaw]. Recovering from the initial shock, he smiled at Amalia Dorothea and got out of his chair. He extended his right hand: "Thank you Frau von Eichendorff Dingdong!" Apfelbaum followed suit with his gesture of gratitude. Holding her head high, her back as straight as she was taught as a young girl, Amalia merely smiled as she walked out of the station, leaving her two charming gentlemen in blue behind—staring into infinity. Apfelbaum and Sattler wondered what thoughts the great lady carried away with her.

Acknowledgments

THE author wishes to express his sincere gratitude to Graham Schofield for his invaluable critical support and suggestions during the editorial process of this work. Expressions of great appreciation are extended to the staff of Wheatmark Publishing Services for their efforts in bringing the Birken Trilogy to fruition. Special recognition is accorded to Wheatmark's Senior Project Manager, Lori Conser, for her dedicated and diligent work leading to the publication of the author's writings. Many thanks are due those who have encouraged the author to write, in particular the members of the Green Valley Writers' Forum and family and friends. Last but not least, the author recognizes his wife, Lynne, with heartfelt thankfulness for her endless hours of reading and providing critical editorial commentary.